ALSO BY HANNAH JAYNE

Truly, Madly, Deadly
See Jane Run
The Dare

THE ESCAPE

HANNAH JAYNE

sourcebooks
fire

Published by Sourcebooks Fire, an imprint of Sourcebooks, Inc.
P.O. Box 4410, Naperville, Illinois 60567-4410
(630) 961-3900
Fax: (630) 961-2168
www.sourcebooks.com

Library of Congress Cataloging-in-Publication Data is on file with the publisher.

Printed and bound in United States of America.
VP 10 9 8 7 6 5 4 3 2 1

To Cyrus Yocum—for seeing me.

ONE

"Come on, loser!" Adam yelled over his shoulder.

Fletcher could hear Adam's laughter echoing back at him as he pumped his legs, intent on keeping the deep green of Adam's jacket in sight as he dodged through the forest.

There was no way Fletcher could catch Adam unless Adam stopped or dropped dead. Adam was the quarterback who brought Dan River Falls High School victory after victory, and Fletcher was the "weird kid" who sat at the back of the bleachers and drew in his notebook.

"Come on!"

A second wind broke through Fletcher's chest, and he felt the burn of adrenaline rush through his legs. He fisted his hands as the cool air dried the sweat on his forehead. A loopy smile cracked across his face. He could see Adam. He was gaining on him—not fast, but steadily. Adam was caught in the crosshairs of Fletcher's gaze.

"Who you calling 'loser'?" Fletcher called, still grinning.

Up ahead, Adam stopped, head bent, shoulders heaving as he

struggled for breath. He was doubled over, staring at something on the ground. "My God, Fletch. Dude, you've got to see this."

• • •

It was just after six o'clock as Avery watched pink bleed into the sunny blue sky, casting a haze of twilight over the parking lot at the Dan River Falls Police Station. The cup of coffee that sat in front of her—more vanilla creamer than coffee—had long since gone cold.

A man strode into the room, his black uniform pressed so each crease was razor sharp. He was no-nonsense from head to toe: salt-and-pepper hair cut close to his skull, dark eyes focused, thin lips pressed together in a scowl. He walked past Avery and dropped a thick manila file folder on the giant desk.

"Dad," Avery moaned, pulling out the word. "Can we go yet?"

Chief Templeton looked at his daughter as if just noticing her—as if she hadn't been sitting there in that same spot for the last forty minutes.

"The line is going to be out the door. I'm going to starve to death while we wait."

"Not now, Avery."

"Fine. Then we're hitting the drive-through with the lights and siren on. I'm pretty sure my stomach is eating itself."

"Your stomach eating itself? Not happening, Avy."

"It happens! We talked about it in biology." It was a lie. Avery had no idea whether or not the stomach could or would eat itself. But it felt like it. She was going to launch into some other wild story to make the stern police chief crack a smile and bring him back to acting like her dad. But when he turned, Avery could see that there was no playfulness in his eyes. His lips weren't going to quirk up into a smile no matter how hard she tried. She swallowed, fear inching up the back of her neck.

"What's wrong, Dad?"

• • •

He couldn't remember the first blow, though his teeth were still rattling in his head. Had he been punched, shot, hit? His vision was a blur, and everything around him, every tree, every rock, seemed to blend together in one united mass of gray. He wasn't sure if the sky was above or below him, if the trees were standing or if he was.

Another blow.

The pain was dense at first, then exploded into a blinding burn. He blinked, dumbfounded, and tried to face his attacker. But his body was leaden. It was as if his feet were rooted in the soft blanket of pine needles on the damp forest ground. He knew he should roll his fingers into a fist and take a swing, but while his brain worked, his body didn't. Thoughts of action tossed around in his skull—run, yell, fight, punch—but everything moved in sickly slow motion except for the terror that overwhelmed him.

I'm going to die.

The thought came to him with a sickening dread.

I don't want to die.

Then came a gruesome thud followed by a sharp crack. The sound filled his ears before he registered that it was his bones breaking. *Snap, crack.* He knew another blow was coming and he tried to brace himself, balling up, wondering if the next hit would be the one that killed him.

TWO

"Adam Marshall and Fletcher Carroll," Chief Templeton replied.

Avery shrugged. "What about them?"

Adam Marshall was a jock at Dan River Falls High. He was a junior, a grade older than Avery, but she knew him—everyone did. Generally, Avery studiously avoided jocks and great-at-everythings, but Adam was different. Avery and Adam had been friends as kids, playing on the baseball diamond back when boys and girls and popularity didn't matter. Maybe that was why he was nice to her now. He smiled at her, calling her by name. He ushered along the mean girls when they were poised to pick apart whatever shred of confidence Avery had.

Adam was everything Fletcher Carroll wasn't. While Adam was a beacon of light with white-blond hair and a Crest-toothpaste smile, Fletcher was always hunched in his hoodie, hiding behind a mass of thick brown curls that were a half inch too long to be considered fashionably shaggy. Avery and Fletcher were neighbors. He was nice enough, but he kept to himself. He was the kind of kid who didn't really fit in but didn't really stick out either.

Chief Templeton drummed his fingers on his desktop, the sound like the rat-a-tat-tat of machine-gun fire. "They went hiking this morning and haven't come back yet."

Avery shrugged. "So?"

"So they were supposed to be back three hours ago. Fletcher's mother is here; she wants to file a report. Adam's parents are on their way as well."

"They've only been gone a few hours," Avery said. "They probably got drunk and passed out in a clearing."

Chief Templeton raised his eyebrows. "Is that what you kids do out there?"

Avery rolled her eyes. "Not 'us kids,' *some* kids. Some of us starve to death because our fathers promise cheeseburgers that never materialize."

But Avery's dad wasn't listening. He stared over her head at the graying sky. A little niggle of fear started at the base of Avery's spine, and she shifted in her seat to follow his gaze to the thick clutch of pine trees off in the distance. If it was gray here, it had to be near pitch-black out in the woods.

"It's too early to really be worried, isn't it, Dad?"

• • •

He was thirsty. His lips were burning, and his throat was raw from screaming. His head pounded so severely that his vision would darken and then snap back to clear before fading again.

He couldn't make out where he was.

He could feel the cold earth cradling him, a soft blanket of pine needles haloing behind his head. A multitude of scents bombarded him as he struggled to gain awareness: the biting scent of pine, the mossy smell of dirt, and something else. Something metallic and cloying. He tried to turn his head, but it was immobile like his limbs. If he could see properly, he could figure out what was holding him down and pressing the breath from his chest. If he could move, even just an inch, maybe he could get away. But all he could do was take in a glimpse of the darkening sky each time his vision cleared.

Not far away, a few feet maybe, he could hear footsteps. At least he hoped they were footsteps, not some bear or whatever had walloped him into his current supine state. The crunch of dry leaves and popping twigs was getting closer. He was sure of it. A wave of primal fear coursed through him. As his adrenaline surged, he dug his fingertips into the dirt around him. *If I can push myself up*, he thought, *at least then I won't be a sitting duck.*

Though his spine felt as if it had been snapped in two, he pushed himself up with a slow groan that became a strangled, gurgling sound. Blood filled his mouth and trickled out his nose. Sweat bulleted his forehead and the thrum in his head grew more severe, like a talon in his skull, raking against the bone.

He tried to cradle his aching head, but one arm screamed in pain while the other fell at his side, useless, his elbow bending the wrong way. His stomach went to liquid at the sight of his own wounds, and he vomited, spit and blood and puke splattering the dirt next to him.

When he fell back again, the blue above had turned into the blackest night.

THREE

Avery could hear her father rustling around before the sun rose. She pushed herself out of bed and dressed quickly. She didn't need to ask what had happened—she already knew.

Her father had been the Dan River Falls chief of police since Avery was fifteen. That was the last year her family had been all together. One of her favorite memories was when they rode in the Founder's Day parade. The chief's black-and-white SUV had been wrapped with red, white, and blue crepe-paper streamers, and she and her mother had practiced waving delicately, her mother's lips upturned in a permanent smile.

Avery remembered the way her father had pulled her mother close, just before they turned onto the parade route. His fingers had tangled in her chestnut-brown hair as he kissed her. When they'd pulled away, her parents had both laughed. Her prim and pressed father had now sported bright red lips, a transfer of her mother's lipstick. Avery had groaned or gagged at her parents' unbelievably gross public display of affection, though secretly she'd liked that they were always touching, always smiling.

The next year, Avery and her father had ridden in the same car in the parade, but this time in silence. It was just the two of them driving slowly behind the marching band. Avery's mother's absence had been palpable, and Avery had gritted her teeth the whole time, trying to force a smile, knowing her father was doing the same thing.

After a few more blocks, the parade would be over, and Avery and her father would pretend they weren't watching for the clock to strike eight seventeen, the moment Caroline Templeton had been struck by a drunk driver on her way home from the Founder's Day barbeque, the moment she had been killed.

Avery's father had the coffee going and his travel mug out, so Avery started breakfast, pulling out a carton of eggs and the frying pan.

"No word on—"

Her father shook his head and filled both mugs, fixing hers with enough milk and sugar to turn it a pale brown while leaving his black. He screwed the lids on both, then took a sip and dropped two pieces of bread in the toaster as Avery cracked two eggs.

"No word. Green and Howard went in last night just before sunset but didn't see anything."

"Nothing?"

"Car was in the lot. Last one there. As far as we know, neither boy contacted anyone at home or any friends."

The toast popped up and Chief Templeton slathered each slice with butter, laying them on separate paper towels.

Avery flipped the eggs. "Well, if neither of them made contact, that could be a good sign, right? They're probably together."

The chief salted and peppered the eggs over Avery's shoulder. She nudged him out of the way and slipped a fried egg onto each slab of toast. He handed her a bright-orange Windbreaker; she handed him one of the egg sandwiches.

"You know you're basically just keeping the kids out of the way, right?" The chief's tone was calm, but his eyes were wary.

Avery stiffened. She had been on more missing-person searches—unofficially, as she was underage—than most of the officers on her father's staff. But being sixteen kept her on "kid patrol," basically babysitting while the adult volunteers tromped through the forest, potentially ruining scads of evidence while pretending they were a bunch of television CSIs, no doubt.

"Yeah," she said through a mouthful of fried egg. "I know."

He chucked her shoulder. "Don't be like that. When you're of age, you can show off your detective skills. Until then, we do things by the book."

Avery looked away, thinking about her mother, about how she would zing the chief in the ribs and remind him not to be so serious. "By the book," she would mock in a terrible baritone. "I'm the big, bad chief."

Avery let out a tight sigh. "I know, Dad. By the book."

• • •

Is this what it feels like to die?

He wheezed, imagining his breath leaving his body around jags of broken bones and swollen flesh. He didn't really know what was broken and what was swollen, but judging by the pain, he guessed everything. He tried to swallow and winced when saliva laced with

11

blood slid down his throat. His head hadn't stopped pounding and his stomach lurched.

He turned his head to the side, ignoring the twigs that dug into his cheek. Eyes closed, he vomited. He kept them closed—not at the pain, but in an effort to avoid seeing his innards, which he was sure he was spitting up. Then everything went black.

• • •

Avery was leaning over, tightening her hiking boots, when she heard the voice that set her teeth on edge. It was Kaylee Cooper, a girl who sported a wardrobe full of pink, fuzzy sweaters and cheerleading skirts that barely covered her butt. She was goddess-like and blond, with hair that nipped at her waist, and eyes that looked sweetly innocent until they narrowed and her gaze sliced you into ribbons. She was popular for being either a tease or a slut, Avery couldn't remember which, and she never moved without a swarm of girls orbiting her. They all looked the same, interchangeable, one popping into the Kaylee system as another fell away.

"Is this where we meet for the hike?" Kaylee asked Avery's arched back.

Avery straightened. "It's not a hike. It's a missing-person search. And yes." She handed Kaylee a clipboard. "Sign in here, please."

She watched as Kaylee produced a pink-and-white pen and signed her name with a flourish and hearts. *A flourish and hearts*, Avery thought, *while two kids are out in the woods, possibly injured, possibly dead.*

She shook her head at the annoyance that overwhelmed her and slipped on her bright-orange search-and-rescue jacket. It didn't take long for a group to form behind her, mainly kids from school, including Kaylee and her admirers. When Officer Vincent Blount came over to explain the details of the search, Avery hugged her arms across her chest, her feet tapping.

She was anxious to get into the woods. Though her conversations with Adam had dwindled as the years passed until they were virtual strangers in high school, he *had* asked her for geometry help. She'd been surprised and thrilled when they'd met in the library and he'd hung on her every word. They'd talked in hushed tones for hours—not about geometry but about everything, until the sun set and the librarian whisked them out. Outside on the sidewalk, he'd leaned in and she could smell the soap he used and his cologne and shampoo. Avery had thought Adam was going to kiss her then and there—but Kaylee had pulled up in her stupid new car and the moment had been ruined.

Now the teen search group filed into lines and started down the trail Adam and Fletcher would have walked. Avery took slow, deliberate steps, calling out the boys' names, the voices of the other volunteers nearby swallowed up by the foliage. Avery wasn't sure how long they walked, but they were deep enough into the forest that the overgrowth blocked out most of the sunlight and the temperature had dropped more than a couple of degrees.

She zipped her jacket and stepped away from the group—a cardinal sin, she knew—and headed toward a small bit of earth that looked to have been recently tromped through. She glanced over her shoulder at her group; they were taking a break. Most were drinking from water bottles or sitting in the dirt. No one seemed to miss her. She looked around and saw a path marked by more broken twigs, winding deeper into the forest, deeper into the shadows.

It was impossibly quiet where she was, as if the thick, leafy canopy snuffed out the outside world completely. The result was an eerie stillness that gave Avery goose bumps and sent a quiver through her stomach. A twig snapped behind her and she spun. Her body stiffened like an animal ready to pounce. Then came the rustle of pine needles.

• • •

It was back. It—he—whatever or whoever had done this to him was back, probably to finish him off. A tremor of terror rolled through him, each miniscule quiver making his bones crack all over again.

Just kill me. Just kill me and get this over with.

The only part of his head that didn't feel like it was stuffed with cotton pounded behind his eyes. The blood pulsing through his ears blocked out every other sound, but he thought he could hear the whisper of someone trying to get his attention.

Let him kill me.

He couldn't run, couldn't even stand, but something like hope pushed through him

No.

The footsteps grew more distinct. A crunch of leaves, weight on the hard-packed earth.

I don't want to die.

He could feel the tears warm his cheeks, and he gritted his teeth against the explosion of pain as he inched himself backward under a bush to hide.

Don't let it get me.

• • •

"Hello?" she called out. "This is Avery Templeton with Search Team Five. Hello?"

The silence was complete except for the steady thump of Avery's heart. She took a step forward and slid on the loose earth, tumbling forward onto her hands and knees. Rocks tore at her skin and the knees of her jeans as she slid. When she stopped—eight, ten feet at the most—she was breathing heavily, her mind reeling. She did a quick assessment for damage. Other than the sting on her palms, nothing hurt.

So why was there blood on her hands?

She brought her hands toward her face and grimaced at the streaks of rust-colored blood—congealed, mixed with dirt—that covered her palms.

She wasn't bleeding.

This wasn't her blood.

It was then that she heard the slow gurgle, the sparse intake of breath followed by a low, throaty whisper: "Avery, you have to help me."

Avery stared at the figure lying in front of her, allowing her eyes to adjust to the dim light.

"Please."

The word came out in a desperate hiss, and he clasped a muddy, blood-caked hand around her wrist, his grip limp, his fingers trembling.

She gasped. "Fletcher?"

FOUR

"Oh my God, Fletcher!"

Avery wouldn't have noticed him but for the white of his right eye. His left was swollen shut, the purple skin stretched so tight that it was glossy, and his face was caked with dirt and dried blood. More blood congealed at his hairline and along his part, matting his curly hair.

Avery tried to focus on his good eye rather than his broken body and the putrid stink of sick and sweat.

"Can you hear me okay?"

Fletcher made a motion that could have been a nod, his head moving almost imperceptibly in the dirt.

"Are you injured?" she asked, her search-and-rescue training kicking in. "Can you move at all?"

Fletcher's eye cut from left to right and widened like a caged animal's. His tongue slipped from his mouth and traced his cracked lower lip. His eyelids fluttered, and Avery watched as tears pooled underneath his lashes.

"I don't think so," he whispered.

"That's okay. Don't try and move. Here." She unscrewed the cap on her water bottle and gingerly pressed it to Fletcher's lips. He winced as the water dribbled into his mouth. She bit down her fear, ignored the urge to run. If someone did this to Fletcher, where was he? Was he watching her now? Waiting?

Avery set her teeth against the tremble in her voice. "Do you know where Adam is?"

• • •

Adam.

The intense joy Fletcher had felt as Avery's lithe figure kneeled next to him receded. He wasn't alone. He wasn't going to die. But Adam…

His chest tightened and his heart clanged like a fire bell. The pounding was so severe it felt as if it was hammering each of his injured ribs, which made it difficult to breathe.

"Adam." The name felt heavy on his tongue.

Where was Adam?

A tiny sliver of memory came back to him: It was sunny, too hot for a September Saturday. The car windows were rolled down, and even with the wind whooshing by, Fletcher could feel the sun baking his fair skin. Someone was singing—badly—yelling really, to a song on the radio.

Death to Sea Monkeys.

Everyone at school loved that band.

Fletcher hated it.

Who was singing?

Adam.

"Where's Adam?" Fletcher asked.

Fletcher could feel Avery gently touch his shoulder. Hope rose inside him, then broke.

"Do you remember what happened?" she asked.

He closed his eyes. "Someone…someone…hit us." His voice rose on the word "us." It was as much a question as a statement. His mind churned, spitting out broken images: a hand curling into a fist, the shooting pain on its impact, getting knocked off his feet. Yelling, screaming…so much noise. "I don't remember."

Avery pulled out her cell phone. The rectangle of light illuminated her blue eyes and the wispy hairs that stuck out from her ponytail.

"No service." Her eyes flashed. "Don't worry. I'm going to go get help. There are six search teams and my dad can't be more than a mile away." She sprung to her feet. "I'll be right back."

It took all of Fletcher's might not to grab on to Avery. He didn't want her to see him scared, to see him cry, but it was already too late for that. "Don't leave me, Avery, please," he pleaded.

Avery bit her bottom lip, her eyes scanning the little gulley they were in. She looked toward the makeshift trail and tree line. "Do you think whoever did this will come back?" The confidence had dropped out of Avery's voice, and Fletcher could hear the tremor of uncertainty.

Fletcher blinked. *Whoever did this…* Who did this? "I don't know."

"There's no other way, Fletcher. You're injured. If I try to move you, I'm only going to hurt you more. I'll be back—with help—in a few minutes. I promise. I'm not going to leave you out here any longer than I have to. I'll be right back."

Fletcher knew she was right. Even when he told himself to move—to bend a knee, move a finger—nothing happened. His brain and body were disconnected. Avery had to get help.

• • •

Avery didn't realize she was crying until she cleared the edge of the gulley and broke into a run. The cool air breaking over her cheeks went icy on the tracks of her tears. What had happened to Fletcher? Where was Adam? Who had attacked the boys?

A bright-orange snatch of fabric—another rescue worker— flashed through the thinning trees, and she pressed herself harder, knowing she was close, ignoring the tightness in her lungs.

"Dad! Dad! I found him! I found Fletcher! We need an ambulance! Call the paramedics!"

Avery skidded on some damp leaves, and Chief Templeton caught her by her shoulders. "Avery?"

The other members of the chief's search party stared. Nobody moved.

Avery gasped for air.

"Avery?" he repeated.

"Dad, he's alive. Come on."

Chief Templeton straightened. "You heard the girl. Get a stretcher. Call in the search teams! Where is he, Avy?"

She nodded deeper into the woods. "I'll show you."

• • •

The lights burned his eyes. Even when he closed them, yellow starbursts exploded in the darkness and made his head hurt worse. His lips were dry and puckered, and he wished for another sip from Avery's bottle. It was quite possibly the best water he had ever tasted. That seemed like a lifetime ago—being in the forest with Avery. Was there something before that?

There had to be.

He felt like he was gliding. Fletcher's eyes flickered open again. The bright bursts of lights were coming from the ceiling. He was in a hallway. Panicked faces hovered above him. He could see their lips moving, but he couldn't make out what they were saying over the beeping and someone being paged. Everything was muffled, one step removed, as if he had cotton in his ears.

He lifted his head an inch. He could see a thick, yellow strap clamped around his shoulders and the rise and fall of his own chest. The paramedic must have sliced his shirt down the middle. Fletcher's concave stomach, his pasty, un-tanned skin, was exposed. He was going to ask for a blanket or a new shirt, but his tongue was heavy in his mouth. He couldn't make sense of what'd happened, what *was* happening. His mind felt as if it was fraying at the edges. Then it plunged him back into the black.

FIVE

Avery watched the shadows passing across her ceiling, hoping that the monotony would lull her to sleep, but each time the tree branches moved in the wind, her heart fluttered. The house was impossibly quiet, which made each scuff against the stucco outside, each howl of wind, sound that much louder.

Whenever she closed her eyes, she saw Fletcher curled up on the forest floor, his lips chapped, his face bruised and streaked with dried blood. It seemed wrong—horribly so—that the kid who lived practically across the street, whose house Avery had passed on a thousand bike rides, was lying in a hospital bed rather than his own.

And she wondered about Adam.

Avery's father and his group were continuing the search, but the chief had sent her home with Officer Blount at about ten thirty. She had tried to protest, but there was no arguing with him when he had that determined look.

She rolled over to look at the glowing red numbers on her alarm clock: 4:57. She shivered. If Adam was still out there…

A car pulled into the driveway, and Avery listened as the garage door opened. Her father was home. A flitter of nerves coursed through her. Her father would be upset to catch her still awake.

She listened to his footfalls, tracing his routine in her head: The slam of the car door. The whine of the side door opening and closing. The thunk of the chief's gun belt knocking against the washing machine as he walks through the narrow laundry room. The rush of the kitchen faucet as he fills a glass of water. Then heavy footsteps on the stairs.

Avery listened, waiting for the familiar sounds of her father opening his bedroom door, placing his gun belt on the top shelf of his closet, and flopping down on his bed with a sigh that made her heart heavy.

Instead, there was a quick knock on her door.

"Avy?" The chief pushed the door open, letting in the bright light from the hallway.

Avery held a hand over her eyes. "Dad?" She squinted at him. He was still dressed in his uniform, his gun in his holster. "Did you find Adam?"

The look on her father's face made a lump form in Avery's throat. *Was he dead?* She didn't want to ask.

"Not yet." The chief walked into Avery's room and picked up the clothes she had worn that day from the chair where she had left them. He tossed them on the end of her bed. "Get dressed. We're going to the hospital."

Avery pushed off her blankets and swung her feet to the ground. "What? Why?"

"Fletcher's starting to talk. He's beginning to remember some of what happened."

"Okay…but why am I going to the hospital?"

"Because he'll only speak with you." The chief turned without further explanation, shutting Avery's door behind him.

Avery blinked in the darkness before pulling on a pair of sweatpants. Why did Fletcher want to talk to her? Correction: why would he *only* talk to her? She slipped into an old Dan River Falls High sweatshirt, her unease growing, her fingers going to the fabric. She had what her father called "nervous hands," so the sleeves of the dark-purple hoodie—as well as the hems of most of her clothes—were frayed from wear and constant picking.

She gathered her brown hair into a sloppy ponytail. She had gone to bed with it still damp from her shower, so now the strands curled every which way. But she didn't give it a second thought as she pulled on her sneakers and then took the stairs two at a time, meeting her father in the kitchen.

Chief Templeton's face was drawn, the lack of sleep showing in the dark circles under his brown eyes.

"We can grab McDonald's on the way," he said simply, before turning on his heel and heading to the garage.

Avery nodded and followed her father.

In the car, she dutifully clicked her seat belt. Her gaze mimicked his as he checked all his mirrors and put the car into reverse. On better days, he would quiz Avery on what he should do next to prep her for driver's ed next semester. But in the graying light of dawn, they were silent.

Once they pulled into the drive-through, Avery cleared her throat. "What does Fletcher want, Dad?"

The chief shrugged and placed their orders. "He just said he wanted to talk."

"If he just wanted to chat, you wouldn't have pulled me out of bed at five in the morning."

The expression on the chief's face didn't change. He fished a few bills from his wallet.

When they pulled up to the service window, Avery watched her father morph into chief mode, the way he did whenever he was in public. His lips curved into a sure smile, and his eyes shone as he asked about the drive-through woman's morning. He passed Avery the bags of food, and the lady in the window called, "See ya, Chief! See ya, Chief's daughter!" as they pulled away.

"So you don't know why Fletcher wants to speak with you? You guys aren't close or anything, friends at school? I don't think I've ever seen him come over to the house."

"He hasn't. We *go* to school together, so we know each other. I mean, he and his mom practically live across the street. But we're not like, *close* close. Not since we were, like, eleven."

"Did he say anything when you found him?"

Avery shook her head, taking a bite of hash browns and letting the salt, grease, and crunch dissolve in her mouth. "No. Not really."

"He didn't mention anything about Adam, anything about what might have happened to him?"

Again, Avery shook her head. "No. I told you. He said he didn't remember. He had this really weird, vacant look, like he didn't know who Adam was. Maybe it was shock or something."

The chief rolled his car to a stop at a red light and turned to her. "What do you know about Adam?"

"Adam?" She bit into her sandwich, not tasting it. "He's just a regular guy, I guess. Really nice."

"Do you think he would have any reason to hurt Fletcher?"

"You think Adam was the one who did this?"

Her father gave one of those half nods that meant neither no nor yes. "We haven't found Adam yet, and Fletcher's hurt pretty badly."

"Is Adam a suspect?"

"I'm not saying that. Right now Adam is a missing kid who may have been out alone in the woods all night."

Avery balled up the remains of her sandwich, no longer hungry.

"Fletcher's mother called in the missing-person report, but Adam's family was right behind her. Do you know who suggested the hike?"

"Dad, I don't know them like that. We never really talked in school or anything, so no, it's not like we discussed our weekend plans."

Avery's mind flashed back to that time in the library with Adam. The electric feeling of being near him, of him reaching out to touch her cheek, was like hitting your funny bone—strange but not unpleasant. His eyes had been warm and comforting. Just his proximity had made her feel safe. She couldn't imagine Adam turning into a monster.

"I don't think Adam would do that. He's—he's…nice."

Chief Templeton shot Avery a look that practically delivered a lecture of its own, reminding her that bad guys don't always "look" bad and good guys can be the ones you least expect.

Then Avery thought back on when she'd found Fletcher in the woods. His eyes had lost focus, as if his mind had gone *somewhere else* when she asked about the other boy.

Suddenly, Avery's hash browns sat like a hot rock in her gut.

She remembered reading an article about the brain stashing away memories—even recent ones—until the waking mind could process them. Had Adam attacked Fletcher? Or had whatever happened to Adam been so bad that Fletcher's brain had locked away the memory?

• • •

Memories, flashbacks, visions of the woods pierced his sleep like shards of broken glass, tearing holes in his relative calm. In the safety of his hospital room, Fletcher shifted, tossing off the thin blankets, wincing at the explosion of pain the movement caused. He pushed back into his pillow, his breathing raspy and shallow.

The images couldn't have been real. They must have been hallu-cinations, brought on by the medications the doctors had been pumping into his veins since he'd arrived at the hospital. Why else would he have visions of Adam, his face contorted in anger and then lapsing into pure terror? But Fletcher saw his friend clawing at hands that encircled his throat, heard his desperate gasps for air, the breath that called to him—"Fletch." It was like watching film footage of an old horror movie.

What had happened to Adam?

Fletcher glanced at the empty visitor's chair at the side of his bed, glad that his mother had finally gone home. Otherwise, she sat there, wringing her hands and staring at him. He was tired of being stared at.

He looked around the room for a clock, but there wasn't one. He guessed marking time somehow went against the healing process. He wondered when Avery would arrive. He didn't know what he'd say to her, why he'd even asked for her, but when the doctors and officers, even the chief of police, peppered him with questions, his tongue had stuck to the roof of his mouth. That didn't stop them from trying to coax him to talk, saying things that shouldn't come out of adults' mouths like, "It's cool, Fletcher. You can talk to us. We're here to listen."

They didn't get it. They couldn't, because even he didn't get it.

Branches breaking underfoot, slipping in the mud as he ran, cringing, flinching, everything hurting. The smack of skin against skin, knuckles against bone, his palms scraping against rock, the moisture of—What was it? Blood? Damp?—seeping through his jeans as he fell. Adam, Adam, Adam...

SIX

Avery's mouth was dry. What was she supposed to say to him?

"Just listen," Chief Templeton said as though he were reading his daughter's mind. "Just listen to whatever he has to say and be there for him. Like a friend." He offered her a formal smile that must have been reassuring for victims or witnesses or whoever her father normally dealt with, but it only made her feel more uncomfortable.

She nodded. "I guess."

Fletcher and his mother had moved into the neighborhood about five years ago. Avery was ten, just about to turn eleven, a tomboy teetering on the edge between liking boys and wanting to strike them out with her wicked three-fingered fastball.

The first time she had seen Fletcher, he had wandered out into the park, a half-abandoned stretch of grass and weeds with bases and a pitcher's mound scuffed out by the kids who played there. Avery was winding up a pitch, while Adam eyed her, his bat at the ready. A handful of kids were milling on bases or kicking rocks in their makeshift dugout. Fletcher had walked right through the game as if he had no idea anyone was even there.

She thought about that kid now—unaffected, indifferent—and tried to reconcile him with the one she had found in the woods. She thought of Fletcher's eyes, the desperate way they'd looked at her, begging her to notice him on the *forest floor*.

Now Avery stood outside Fletcher's hospital room, her heart thudding in her ears.

Would he be waiting for her? Would he even be awake?

Chief Templeton pushed the door open.

Fletcher was sitting up in his bed, looking out at the sunrise.

Chief Templeton cleared his throat. "Avery's here to talk. I'll be in the hallway if you need me."

Fletcher turned slowly, hunched as though he were an old man.

Avery sucked in a breath. His face was clean now, but the bruises remained. A gash above his eye cut across his forehead and shot toward his scalp, where a quarter-sized chunk of his hair had been shaved away. He was covered in scratches.

Fletcher's smile was lopsided. He gently touched the side of his head. "I probably look really stupid. They wouldn't even let me see a mirror."

"No," Avery said, her cheeks flushing with embarrassment at being caught staring. "You look fine. Good, I mean."

They both knew it wasn't true and stared at each other in uncomfortable silence.

"Do you want to sit down?" Fletcher asked

Avery nodded and slid into the visitor's chair.

They sat in silence for a moment, Avery listening to her careening heartbeat, certain that Fletcher could hear it too. She tried not to stare, but even cleaned up, the wounds on Fletcher's face were bad. She thought about the possibility that Adam could have been the one to do this to Fletcher. It was impossible, she decided finally, absurd. The person who did this to Fletcher—the person who attacked him and Adam—had to be a monster. There was nothing else to it.

• • •

Fletcher watched Avery. Her actions were stiff and self-conscious. So was he. He had never been this close to a girl before. It felt so intimate, him being so vulnerable.

He didn't even know why he had asked for her. It just came out of his mouth while everyone was throwing questions at him. His doctor kept holding his hand out to the officers, warning them that Fletcher's condition could be "touch and go"—that was the phrase he used. But even when the officers backed off, the doctor started in: "Can you move this? Does that hurt? Do you remember if you were hit here…?" It was all a painful, weird blur, memories sharp and faded at the same time.

"I want to talk to Avery," Fletcher had said before the fog had set in. "I want to talk to Avery, please."

Maybe it was because she was kind of a loner like him, or because she had been through something traumatic too. Maybe it was because she had been the one to find him.

A thought played on his periphery but Fletcher didn't want to pay attention to it: had he asked for Avery because she found him or because she saved him?

• • •

"My dad said you wanted to talk to me."

Fletcher's cheeks went red.

"It's okay, you know," Avery continued, nerves humming. She wanted to comfort Fletcher. She wanted to be as good as her dad. But seeing Fletcher in front of her—part friend, part victim—shook her. "You don't have to talk to me. I mean, you don't have to tell me anything. Unless you want to. I won't… It can be between us." She was stammering, her hands flopping in front of her as she talked.

Fletcher opened his mouth, and then he shrugged. His shoulders looked small and bony beneath the oversized hospital gown. He looked fragile beyond the cuts and bruises, and Avery wondered how Fletcher was able to defend himself at all.

He looked down at his lap, his chin on his chest.

"Maybe you could tell me when you guys decided to go hiking. I mean, I didn't know you and Adam really hung out."

Fletcher's head snapped up. "Me and Adam are friends. We hang out." The edge in his voice frightened Avery. Then his face softened. "I'm sorry. I didn't mean to get mad. It's just…you know, people think I'm a geek. And why would someone who is popular like Adam hang out with the geek?"

Except people didn't call Fletcher a geek. They coughed *freak* or *loser* into their hands when he passed or asked a question in school. They called Avery a geek.

Fletcher traced the pattern on his pajamas with his fingernail. "The hike wasn't really anyone's idea. We'd been talking about hiking, checking out the woods, and just got in the car. It's not something we did all the time. We aren't mountain men or anything."

Avery nodded. "Yeah, it's usually a good idea to bring water and a map with you."

"A map?" He laughed. "Care to join us in the digital age, Avery? It's called GPS."

She laughed despite feeling stung. "It's called no cell towers in the forest."

Fletcher reached out, his fingers featherlight on the back of her hand. "And then you found me."

Avery matched Fletcher's small smile, but something felt off.

• • •

We were just going to go for a hike. Nothing big, just a walk in the woods.

"Hey, Fletch. You've got to see this!"

Adam's voice was a subtle call in the back of Fletcher's head, and he squeezed his eyes shut. He could see his own sneakered feet and the tamped-down ground around him. He could feel the wind on his cheeks and see where Adam had stopped up ahead.

And then what happened?

An explosion of white-hot pain shot behind Fletcher's right eye, and his vision went black.

"Hey, Fletch. Hey, are you okay?"

Hey, Fletch…

It was Avery this time and Fletcher wanted to grab her, wanted to hang on to her for dear life. If she wrapped her arms around him, could she keep him here, could she keep him from slipping into the blackness? He tried to speak, but all that came out was a shallow groan.

Fletcher could feel the shift of Avery's weight on the mattress as she moved toward him.

"Should I call the nurse? Are you okay?"

"No, don't," Fletcher panted, the pain shooting waves of nausea into his stomach. "I'm okay." The pain started to subside.

He remembered the doctor's fingers on his scalp, gently feeling along his forehead until he yelped at the same explosion of pain. The doctor had rattled off notes to the nurse: *cranial damage, frontal lobe injury.*

Avery stared at him, her eyes intense. "Fletch?"

"I'm sorry. I… Sometimes there are these…pains."

She cocked her head, her eyebrows diving into a concerned V. "You look like you took a pretty big hit."

Fletcher watched Avery's fingers—delicate and slim—brush a lock of hair from his face. The light pressure from her fingers over his forehead sent a shiver through him.

"Does it hurt much?"

"Yeah. But the pain, the headaches, I mean… I've had those before."

Avery's hands dipped back into her lap and Fletcher went on.

"I guess I hit my head pretty badly." He gingerly touched the zigzag of stitches that crossed his hairline. "Or whatever hit me."

"Do you know? Do you have any—"

Fletcher shook his head. "I start to remember and then… there's nothing."

Avery looked toward the door. "After…after I lost my mom, it was that way for me too." She swallowed the lump in her throat.

"Sometimes I couldn't even remember what she looked like. All I could see was…" She shuddered.

Fletcher vaulted back to the Founder's Day celebration that summer. That night he had felt a part of something, a part of *them*. The whole school—the whole town—was there, and everyone seemed happy, accepting.

They were walking from the celebration. He remembered the sound of Adam's voice reverberating through the trees as he and some other kid hollered and laughed about something. How Avery looked walking along, her hands in the pockets of her shorts. A bunch of other kids was there too, and Fletcher was right in the thick of them as they walked the shoulder of the forest road. Then he remembered the moment when everything changed.

They came around the curve in the road, and it was like stepping into a new scene in a movie: the stinking smell of gasoline and burnt rubber and something else that hung in the night air—something he couldn't place. Then Avery's face was illuminated by the flashing red-and-blue lights of the police cars stopped on the side of the road. He saw the careless smile fall from her lips. Recognition flit through her eyes and then anguish so deep that he could practically feel her pain.

Avery took off running toward the hissing chunk of twisted metal balanced on the edge of the road, one single tire raised to the sky.

It was a car.

Fletcher recognized it as the car that Avery's mother had been driving.

He could still hear Avery's cry. He could still see her fingers grabbing at the air as one of the officers tried to hold her back. But Avery got past him and scudded to her knees on the asphalt, digging at the car. Someone else grabbed her and she screamed. At some point Chief Templeton arrived, and Fletcher remembered the silent exchange between Avery and her father as he pulled her toward his police cruiser. Avery looked at Fletcher then, their eyes locking for one aching minute, her world crashing down, his standing still.

Fletcher ran his tongue over the front of his teeth, anxiety burning in the pit of his stomach. "Did you ever have blackouts? You know, about that night?"

He watched Avery's hands clasped in her lap. Her fingernails were bitten to the quick. He had never noticed that before. She cleared her throat. "Sometimes. I don't know if they were really blackouts though. Just…"

"Dark spots?"

She nodded carefully. "Yeah, some details fade in and out. Or I start to wonder if something I know happened actually did. I heard that the brain can block out things that it can't deal with."

They were both silent for a moment. Then Fletcher spoke. "Do you ever wonder what it feels like to die?"

• • •

Avery's eyes widened. "No."

But she was only telling half the truth. After her mother died, Avery thought about those last few minutes of her mother's life, wondering what her mom was thinking, what she must have felt.

Did she know she was dying? Did she wish for more time? Did she think of Avery?

Even now, it made Avery tear up. She tried not to think about her mother or death.

"I can't help but wonder what happens during…and after." Fletcher looked at her as if he expected her to have the answers. "Do you?" he asked. "Wonder?"

Avery opened her mouth to answer, but there was a knock on the door. Chief Templeton poked his head in. "Avery? Can I see you for a minute?"

• • •

Fletcher didn't want Avery to leave, but he had no reason to ask her to stay. He couldn't remember anything important from the woods, details he knew she was hoping he'd share. And even when he wasn't banged and stitched up, Fletcher had never been a great conversationalist. He offered her a small smile and feigned a yawn. "I should probably get some rest," he said.

Avery stood from the chair and nodded. "Okay. That's probably a good idea." She turned and paused, scrawling something on a piece of paper before handing it to Fletcher. "This is my cell number. Call me if you ever want to talk. Not just about"—she waved her arm indicating the hospital room—"but whatever."

Fletcher took the paper. No girl had ever given him her number before, and although he was certain it had more to do with his injuries than her interest in him, he was okay with it.

He waved as Avery closed the door behind herself, and he sunk back in his pillows. For the first time in as long as he could remember, he smiled. His eyes were heavy, but he didn't want to fall asleep. He didn't want to have another fragmented dream, but even more, he didn't want to forget the sweet smile on Avery's face.

• • •

Avery and her father walked down the hospital corridor in silence. When they got into the elevator, Avery turned to him, arms crossed in front of her chest. She suddenly felt protective of Fletcher after seeing him dwarfed in that hospital bed, his face and body ravaged. She was annoyed that her father would make her a go-between.

"So you want the breakdown?" she snapped. "Because he didn't say much."

"Avery," her father said quietly, "we found Adam." He pushed the button for the parking level, and the car started moving.

Fear fluttered in Avery's chest. "Is he okay? Does he remember anything? Are you going to tell Fletcher?" She paused. "The last two nights were freezing. How long was he out there? He must have hypothermia. Why are we leaving if he's here? I want to see him. You know, to say hey."

A long silence followed. Avery could tell her father was taking his time, letting her get out all of her questions. But the silence stretched too long.

"Dad?"

Her father reached out and squeezed her hand. "Avy, honey," he said quietly. "One of the search teams found Adam in the woods. He's dead. They found his body."

SEVEN

"What?"

The elevator doors slid open to the parking garage, and her father guided her toward his black SUV. He must have helped her into the car and buckled her seat belt, because Avery couldn't remember doing it herself. All she could think about was the empty ache that pulsed through her body.

"Adam's dead?" Images flashed in her mind: Adam in his letterman's jacket. Adam walking through the library, a grin like sunshine, and Avery's heart melting into her shoes. Adam was a boy she had a crush on. Adam was a boy she wanted to kiss. Now Adam was dead. "What—what happened?"

"We're not sure yet. The ME's report isn't ready, and of course the—"

She pressed her fingers on her dad's arm. "In civilian, Dad. Did you see him? What happened?"

His voice was gentle. "I didn't see him personally, Avy. And we're still waiting on a positive ID from his mother."

"But they know it's him."

"They're pretty sure it's him. The sex and height are right."

"Dad, Adam's and Fletcher's faces have been posted all over the news. You know what he looks like. I know you can't make an official statement, but I'm your daughter, not CNN."

The chief ran his hands through his graying crew cut. "Honey, the body was in pretty bad shape."

Avery's stomach rolled and she felt tears prick at the backs of her eyes. Déjà vu pelted her. She and her father had been sitting in this same car two years earlier when her father had said the same words: *The body was in pretty bad shape.* At the time, "the body" was her mother. She had hated him for calling her mother "the body." She had hated him for making her mother generic. *She wasn't a body,* Avery had wanted to scream. *She was my mother!*

"W-what happened to him?"

Adam had been missing for almost two days, and Avery braced herself for the worst. Her father always grunted through crime shows when TV cops stumbled on a so-called corpse that still looked pristine four or five days after death. From his place on the couch, he would explain in clinical—and often gross—detail that "decomp begins four minutes after death."

Avery knew that rigor mortis set in after just a few hours and that Adam's skin would have paled as blood pooled in the lowest points of his body. She knew that if the body had been left unattended in the woods, there would be blowflies and maggots and any other manner of scavenging insects or animals. She tried to shake the images out of her head, but she still needed to know.

"Avy…" Her dad cocked his head, and Avery knew he was trying to placate her.

It was bad.

"Please, Dad?"

The chief gripped the wheel and squinted as he guided the car out of the garage and into the startlingly bright daylight. "He was beaten, and quite a ways away from where they found Fletcher."

Fletcher's voice thrummed in Avery's ears: *They didn't find me, Avery. You did.*

"It sounds as if the blows he sustained killed him. His head—his face… He was barely—" The chief grimaced and shifted in his seat, not bothering to finish his sentence.

Avery had never seen her father, a seasoned police officer, look so saddened and disgusted by a crime. She knew it had to be worse than he was letting on.

"Do you know who did it? Was there any evidence to—"

He held up a silencing hand. "It's an ongoing investigation."

Avery bristled. "I went to school with Adam. We played baseball when we were kids."

Her father let out a small, mirthless laugh. "You guys are still kids."

• • •

Two hundred forty-two.

There were two hundred forty-two tiles on the ceiling of Fletcher's hospital room. He'd counted them. Twice. It felt like forever since Avery had left, and he was bored.

Well, if he was being honest with himself, he was scared.

Whoever had done this to him and Adam was out there, waiting. What was to guarantee that the sneakers squeaking up and down the hallway were nurses' shoes and not the footsteps of his attacker coming for him? It was just a matter of time.

A guard was posted outside his room, but fear crashed through Fletcher in waves, making him sweat.

The door opened and a nurse and an orderly walked in, shuffling papers and massaging IV bags while talking. Fletcher pretended to sleep. He hoped that the heart-rate monitor clamped to his finger wouldn't give his ruse away.

He watched them though slit lids. They were the same two who had been in earlier that morning.

"I heard he was barely recognizable," the nurse said, her voice hushed and anxious. "They could barely tell it was him."

Fletcher's heartbeat raced. He strained to listen as blood pulsed in his ears. *Who are they talking about?*

"That's terrible. I guess this kid was lucky."

"Such a shame. It's a real tragedy. Who would do such a thing to children?" There was a tremor in the nurse's voice. "This town has always been so friendly, so safe. Now I'm afraid to walk to my car at night."

"The police'll catch 'em," the orderly responded. "That Chief Templeton is all over it. They'll find the guy."

Fletcher opened his eyes with the click of the door closing. He let out the breath he didn't know he had been holding.

Did they find Adam? Something twitched in Fletcher's stomach and he wanted to sit up, to get the orderly and nurse back, but something—maybe whatever it was that was slipping through the needle in his arm—weighed him down and kept him quiet. He sank back into his bed, his mind wandering.

The light was starting to change around him, the tops of the pine trees fading into the darkness. They looked like big paintbrushes. Somewhere far away were the rush of water and the gentle rustle of dry leaves. Closer to him was a gurgling sound, occasionally punctuated by a raspy attempt at breath.

He knew he should turn and look at Adam. He knew he should move and get his friend help, but his body wasn't his anymore. It was heavy and useless. The soft earth cradled him like a coffin. His breathing was shallow and sent a thousand burning spikes into his lungs.

Fletcher heard the sound of gravel crunching, of twigs breaking. He strained to see, but it was becoming more difficult to stay awake. And then—there was nothing.

Fletcher half expected the machines attached to him to go haywire with chirps and beeps, signaling that his pounding heart was going to give out, but the machines made no sound. He tried to blink away the memory, but his fingers twitched just the way they had out there in the woods when Adam was close enough to touch—close enough to help.

Fletcher tried to swallow the lump in his throat. The sound of Adam's raspy breath was heavy in his ears. He should have helped. He should have *done* something.

"Fletcher, honey?" His mother knocked while opening the door— just as she had his whole life. She never waited to be invited in.

Her voice was cheerful and light, but she wore a sad smile. Her ashy-blond hair was combed in its usual neat bob, and her milky-blue eyes peered at Fletcher, as if she could take his vital signs just by looking at him. "I brought you some real food."

Fletcher didn't feel hungry, but he couldn't remember the last time he'd eaten. His stomach growled, the sound making his mother smile. She held out a brown cardboard box and opened the top. The aroma of burgers and fries immediately overtook the sanitized odor of the hospital room.

"That smells amazing," Fletcher said. He sat up. "Is Dad coming?"

His mother fixed an apologetic smile on her face. "Oh, he wanted to be here for you. He really did."

Fletcher nodded as grief welled in his chest. They had all been one big, happy family once—Fletcher; his sister, Susan; and their parents. But Fletcher and his mother had moved out and into the house in Avery's neighborhood. It was just across town from his sister and father, but far enough away. Right now, Fletcher couldn't remember why they had moved.

"Burger?" His mother was holding up a sandwich wrapped in yellow paper.

He smiled. "Yeah."

Fletcher was halfway through the burger and a quarter of the way through his chocolate shake when he stopped chewing. "Is it true they found Adam? I heard one of the orderlies talking with a nurse. Can I go see him?"

Mrs. Carroll stiffened, the shock evident on her face.

Fletcher popped a few fries into his mouth. "Didn't they tell you? I thought it would be all over the news."

She cleared her throat. "It has been, honey. Have you seen the news?"

Fletcher shook his head and continued eating. "No. No TV in this room."

His mother smoothed the pleats of her skirt. "Fletcher, honey, you can't see Adam."

Fletcher looked up and furrowed his brow. "Why? Is he in ICU or something? I know I'm not family, but I bet the nurses would still let me in."

Mrs. Carroll didn't respond.

"Ma?" Fletcher said impatiently. "Mom?"

She grimaced. "Fletcher, honey, they found Adam." She cleared her throat. "They found Adam's body."

EIGHT

The news about Adam's death spread like a stain through the school. Students with puffy eyes huddled together, talking in hushed tones. It could have been Avery's imagination, but they all seemed to be looking over their shoulders, even with the addition of two police officers walking the perimeter of the high school. A killer was on the loose, and though one student had escaped, another hadn't. Any one of them could be next.

Avery closed her locker and started when Ellison Rose smiled at her. "Hey, Avery. How you doing?"

Avery counted Ellison as one of her only friends at Dan River Falls High. She was the kind of friend who was close enough to call up, so Avery's father wouldn't think she was a poorly adjusted social outcast, but kept her distance enough to not ask about Avery's mother or anything deep.

"Okay, I guess."

"I was going to—"

"Hey, E." Ellison's boyfriend, a bulky football player named

Tim, slung an arm around Ellison and gave her a loud, smacking kiss on the cheek. "I'm missing my girl."

Ellison looked momentarily torn between Avery and Tim, then tossed a "We'll talk later, okay?" over her shoulder as Tim guided her down the hall.

Avery watched them disappear into the crowded hall but couldn't understand it—the numbing aftermath of death yet the way the world just went on. There were grief counselors but she avoided them, walking down the hallway to her next class. In front of her, a blond with a shoulder-skimming ponytail leaned in to her friend. "I was supposed to babysit my little sister tonight, but now I'm, like, no way. The guy may have been in the woods but he's probably down here in town now, right?"

Avery slipped into her classroom before the other girl could answer, relieved to be away from the chatter. The classroom desks had been rearranged into a loose circle, and Ms. Holly leaned against her desk. Avery prayed they were going to have a flippant conversation about *Huckleberry Finn* or the latest drinking scandal, but when she saw the box of Kleenex going around the room, she knew the conversation would be about Fletcher and Adam. She sat at one of the desks just as the bell rang. Tim sauntered in a moment later.

Ms. Holly stood up. "All of you probably know by now that Adam Marshall's body was found early this morning in the woods. He was deceased. Fletcher Carroll remains in the hospital and is very lucky to be alive. There is no news on exactly what happened or who is responsible." Her eyes flicked to Avery. "Is that correct, Avery?"

Avery shrugged, unwilling to add to the conversation.

"It's terrifying," Kaylee said, pressing a tissue to her perfect little ski-jump nose. "I was out with the search-and-rescue team looking for Adam. I was walking out in the forest while a killer and a dead body were out there. The killer could have seen me." She splayed a perfectly manicured hand against her chest and sniffed into her Kleenex.

Avery laid her head on her desk, trying to block out Kaylee's center-of-the-universe voice.

"There's a murderer out there," Kaylee went on, "a serial killer." She looked around, her flat, blue eyes glossy from the tears. "He could be after any one of us."

Tim leaned forward. "Don't serial killers always have a type though? Adam and Fletcher didn't look that much alike, but they were both boys, both the same age." He pressed a hand against his chest, and Avery couldn't tell if he was serious or joking. "Dude, I could be next."

"Is it true? Do serial killers have a type?" The kid next to Avery poked her with the eraser end of his pencil.

Avery pulled the sleeves of her sweatshirt over her hands, using her thumb and forefinger to roll the fabric back and forth. "How should I know?"

"Your dad's the chief of police," the kid said, as if the connection was obvious.

Avery shrugged.

She *did* know that most serial killers had a type. She also knew that no one in the news or on the police force had mentioned the words "serial killer," and even if they had, the term would be a misnomer. Killers didn't become "serial killers" until they had at least three victims. Whoever did this was just a killer. Yet Avery's spine stiffened at the thought of another kid as bruised and battered as Fletcher, hooked up to hospital monitors.

"What are we supposed to do?" Kaylee asked, tears rolling over her cheeks. "The police are supposed to keep us safe. Why haven't they found this guy?"

Avery felt her nostrils flare and kept rolling the sweatshirt fabric between her fingers to calm herself.

"How was this guy even able to attack Adam and Fletcher in the first place?"

Kaylee stared at Avery. They all did, expecting an answer because she was the police chief's daughter. But she had wondered the same thing.

"Class, we know how to keep ourselves safe. Lock your doors, use the buddy system—"

"The buddy system didn't work out so well for Adam and that other kid," Tim said bitterly.

"Fletcher," Avery said under her breath.

"Avery?" Ms. Holly asked. "Did you say something?"

"The other kid. His name is Fletcher."

"Right. Does anyone feel like they need to talk about Adam, grief, or even death?"

Avery felt like everyone was looking at her again. *Ask Avery. She's the one who went crazy when her mom died*, she imagined them saying. If Ms. Holly asked her to share how it felt to lose someone you love, Avery was going to scream. She clenched her fists.

Kaylee spoke up. "I can't believe I'm never going to see Adam again."

The girl next to her rubbed her back, and Kaylee exploded in delicate tears that wouldn't smudge her makeup. Avery wondered if she had selected her outfit—light-pink top, dark-pink skirt—to accentuate her red cheeks and pink, puffy eyes.

They went around the circle sharing their feelings and memories of Adam, but it was mostly Kaylee talking about loss and prom. Avery simmered in her seat. When Ms. Holly talked about grief counselors and journaling as a way to deal with feelings about loss and death, Avery almost spit out an incredulous laugh. She knew better than any of them. She wanted to tell them what she had learned in the last year: You can't deal with death. It deals with you.

• • •

There was blood all over him. It had dried and made his skin feel so tight that every movement felt like opening a new wound. He'd never thought there would be this much blood. He turned around in a circle, surveying the trees. His heart rate had slowed from its terrified, frenetic pace, but he braced for the moment that his attacker would come back to finish him off.

He didn't know where Adam was. He couldn't remember if Adam ran or was taken, or if he'd escaped. When he saw the streaks across the trail—like from dragging feet—his saliva turned bitter and acrid while the bile filled his mouth.

Fletcher's eyes flew open, and he clawed at the neck of the hospital-issued pajamas he was wearing. He was panting, desperate to breathe, desperate for his body to feel something other than dizzying stress. *What had he dreamed?* He slowly closed his eyes as if doing so would make the memory gentler, but it was the same. He was alone in the forest, covered in blood and left to die.

* * *

Fletcher hadn't had much to say to her when she'd visited, but being at school where he was referred to as "that kid," as in "Adam and *that kid*," bothered Avery. She stepped out of the elevator on Fletcher's floor just as Officer Blount stepped in.

"Hey, Vince. Are you on duty?"

The officer wasn't in uniform, but he wore a black Dan River Falls Police Department T-shirt tucked into black pants, and duty boots laced halfway up his calves. He looked startled to see her.

"Hey, Avery. No, I was just checking in on Fletcher."

"That's really nice of you. Me too." She held up the only thing in the hospital gift shop that wasn't either a fuzzy teddy bear or something decorated with hearts or roses of some sort: a one-pound bag of peanut M&M's. "I brought chocolate."

Blount smiled as he held the elevator door. "I'm sure he'll like 'em. See you later."

Avery's stomach fluttered as she walked toward Fletcher's room. She had no idea what to say to him, and suddenly, a strange girl toting a pound of chocolate for someone she hardly knew seemed ridiculous. She recognized the guard on duty— another of her father's officers—and nodded before knocking on Fletcher's door.

"Avery. Hi." Fletcher moved slowly, his smile crooked due to his swollen bottom lip.

"Wow, Fletch." Dozens of flower bouquets adorned every flat surface in the room. "You're popular."

Fletcher shrugged, his smile fading. "I don't even know most of those people."

Avery wasn't sure how to respond. Then, "I brought you M&M's."

"Thanks."

Avery tucked herself into a chair while Fletcher tore open the M&M's and poured them each a handful.

"I guess you heard about Adam," Fletcher said.

Avery toed the linoleum. "Yeah, I did. Are you okay?"

Fletcher picked out a blue M&M and studied it. "Not really."

"Me neither. But you're alive. That's a good thing."

He looked at her. "I guess. Except Adam was the one everyone loved. He was good at everything."

"Being good at stuff doesn't make one person better than another."

"Still, I'm pretty sure everyone wishes he were the one who had survived."

Avery felt a stab of pain in her chest. "I don't think anyone thinks that, Fletch."

He palmed another fistful of the M&M's, chewing thoughtfully. "Everyone loved Adam. Every teacher, every parent, every student. Even you." His dark eyes settled on Avery's blue ones, and she could feel the heat race to her cheeks.

"We were friends, Adam and me," Avery said. "Like you and me are. Nobody wishes that it had been you. Look at all these flowers."

"No one else has come to visit me. Well, except my mom."

A nurse poked her head in the door. "Visiting hours are over, hon. You're going to have to get going."

Avery waited for the nurse to shut the door. "They probably want to give you your space to rest and feel better. But I'm not the only one who came to visit you. So did Officer Blount. People care about you, Fletcher."

Fletcher blinked, confusion clouding his eyes. "Who's Officer Blount?"

• • •

When Avery rode her bike through town, she noticed ribbon after ribbon in the Dan River Falls High School colors tied around tree trunks, Adam's jersey number puff-painted in glittery silver on the ribbon tails.

There was a makeshift memorial outside the baseball store where Adam worked too. Flowers wrapped in cellophane, teddy bears, handwritten notes, and Kit Kat bars—which Avery guessed must have been Adam's favorite—all held vigil with a number of tall, glass votive candles with Jesus or angels on them.

Avery rode back to the high school and locked her bike in the front rack. Even though the front lot was full of cars and people were milling about, it felt weird to be at school in the evening. Ominous, even.

"Aves!" Ellison was sitting on the stone wall in front of the science building, Tim next to her, thunking his heels on the concrete.

"Hey," Avery said. "I didn't know you guys were going to be here."

Tim unrolled the tube that he was holding. It was a flier. He jabbed a finger at the text. "It's a meeting for the whole town. We"—he gestured to himself and Ellison—"are townsfolk."

"People. We're townspeople, Tim. 'Townsfolk' sounds like we have to be gnomes or something." She turned her attention to Avery. "Did your dad tell you what he would be talking about?"

Avery shifted her weight, suddenly uncomfortable. Ellison looked genuinely curious, but something in Tim's eyes made the hairs on the back of Avery's neck prick. His eyes were clouded, dark—menacing, maybe? Or was he just considering the meeting topic?

"Your guess is really as good as mine. I'm thinking its just details of the case or whatever."

Tim's jaw tightened. "Does your dad have a lead? I mean, they're going to find this guy, right?"

When Avery, Tim, and Ellison walked into the gym, nearly every one of the metal folding chairs was occupied. A few stragglers were leaning against the walls, and a handful of adults stood in front of a folding table where students and the PTA were filling Styrofoam cups with steaming coffee.

Tim and Ellison shimmied through a crowded row and plopped into two seats. Avery remained standing, scanning the crowd.

"We want to assure you that we are doing everything possible to find the person responsible," Chief Templeton said.

Avery headed toward the PTA table and ordered herself a coffee while her father told the community they were in no immediate danger.

She jostled toward the front of the table to pay, bumping into the woolen sleeve of the woman next to her. "Oh, excuse me."

Avery looked up to see Mrs. Marshall with a cup of coffee clutched tightly in both hands, the dazzling blue of her eyes offset by the bags underneath them. Her expression didn't change when she looked Avery up and down. "Hello, Avery."

"Hi, Mrs. Marshall."

They stared at each other for a beat of awkward silence before the chief broke in again, addressing the crowd.

"We have all available officers on high alert, and we assure you that you are safe here in Dan River Falls."

Her father looked confident and professional in his pressed uniform, but an uneasy chatter buzzed through the school gym. Avery cut her eyes toward Mrs. Marshall, who had disappeared into the crowd.

"Can you believe that?" The girl manning the PTA table took Avery's dollar and handed her a steaming coffee. "Just thinking there is a murderer in town scares me to death." The girl shuddered, rubbing her arms as if the cold went all the way through her.

Until that moment, it really hadn't occurred to Avery that the killer could be someone from town. She'd figured it was an outside threat, someone from somewhere else who happened to be in the forest. Evil didn't live in Dan River Falls.

"Yeah." Avery nodded her agreement and took her coffee, half listening to her father and his public information officer quote statistics and field questions from the audience. She scrutinized the crowd, knowing that many murderers like to insert themselves in police investigations and are most often affiliated with their victims.

The problem was that she recognized nearly everyone there. Dan River Falls was a small town. Most people were born, raised, and died within city limits. She couldn't imagine any of them hurting kids like Adam and Fletcher, let alone murdering one of them. But still, she tried to use her sleuthing to weed people out—or in.

An older man that Avery recognized as Fletcher's next-door neighbor was sitting up near her father. He was leaning back in his chair, arms folded across his chest, his expression pensive. There was nothing overtly suspicious about him, but Avery pulled her notebook from her pocket and scrawled down his name anyway. Maybe he had been angry about the boys making noise in the street when they hung out. Maybe he had some sort of vendetta against the Carrolls, and Adam just got in the way.

Avery glanced up at the officers fielding questions and frowned.

"So you're saying that you really have no idea why these boys were targeted, Chief Templeton?"

The question came from a man in the front row, and though her father looked completely confident and comfortable, Avery could see the way his sharp eyes faltered, the almost imperceptible shift of his body at the scornful tone in the questioner's voice.

"We're still figuring out leads and tips, sir, but we're making progress."

Avery had heard that answer a dozen times over the last year and she knew what it meant. They had no idea. She glanced back down at her notepad and the single name written there. Then, in black capital letters, she wrote "WHY" at the top of the page. Why would anyone want to hurt Adam or Fletcher?

She scanned the room a second time, dismissing young kids. She was about to cross off anyone from her school too—she thought there was just no way that someone she'd grown up with and gone to classes with, or who cheered on the Dan River Falls Wildcats, could have done this—but she paused. Especially when she saw who was sitting in one of the back rows.

His name was Jimmy Jerold, and he was the kind of guy every kid feared until they realized that he was just a high-school dropout in a frayed shirt trying to look mean. He had been in and out of juvie since he left school. Avery's father would never tell her exactly, but the rumor was that Jimmy had a mean temper and had broken his own stepfather's nose in a fit of rage.

What if Adam and Fletcher had run into Jimmy and made him mad? Avery tapped her pen against her notepad as her eyes cut to Jimmy and the girl who was sitting next to him. She didn't recognize the blond but Jimmy sure did. He nuzzled the girl's arm and then her chest. The girl clamped her hand over her mouth and giggled, her curls bobbing as she did. Someone turned and shushed them. Jimmy rolled his eyes.

It seemed like a long shot, but her father had always told her that the most obvious answer is usually the right one, so Avery wrote down Jimmy's name with a question mark next to it. As if he knew, Jimmy turned toward Avery, pinning her with his stare, his eyes smoldering and dark. He grinned slowly, rubbing his lips along the girl's arm but never breaking his gaze with Avery.

• • •

"Looks like you have some cracked ribs to go with your broken arm, and other than the cut on your head"—the nurse paused while she looked around the bandage on Fletcher's skull—"nothing overly severe. Should only be another day or two at most."

Fletcher didn't know why that didn't make him happy. He hated being in the hospital—being hooked up to the beeping machines and the constant interruptions from the nurses—but he wasn't sure he wanted to go home. He had been having trouble sleeping, and his eyes felt dry and itchy. Every time he closed them, the dream—or memory, he couldn't figure out which—came back.

The nurse stepped back from his bedside. "How are you feeling? You're looking a lot better, handsome guy." She grinned, but Fletcher knew she was lying. He felt swollen and achy, and he could see the salve glistening on the scratches and cuts on his arms, the spots where his bruises were starting to yellow.

"I'm okay, I guess."

"Are you ready for your meds?" She held a Dixie cup in each hand. She shook the one with the pills in it and grinned. "They will help you sleep."

Sleep. He welcomed heavy and dreamless sleep. No echoes of Adam's voice. No running for safety. No remembering.

Fletcher swallowed the pills and water in a single gulp.

• • •

Avery was only popular when her father was working on a big case. On any *regular* day, she was invisible. But after Adam's body was found and the parade of grief counselors was giving "circle talks" in every classroom, Avery was a celebrity. Everyone wanted to sit with her, to pretend they were friends and had never snubbed her in the halls or at a party. They wanted to know what she knew. They wanted to know about Adam.

"I don't really know anything," she said slowly. "I don't know anything that you guys don't."

Michele, a cheerleader who had orbited Adam for as long as Avery could remember, leaned in. "How do you know we know the same things? Tell us what you know, and we can compare notes."

The students—strangers, really—at her lunch table nodded in agreement. Avery could feel the burn of embarrassment on her cheeks, followed by the sting of anger. For two days, kids had been slinging their arms over her shoulders asking if she was okay. For two days, teachers had tentatively dropped test papers and home-work assignments on her desk, breathily whispering things like, "if you can't manage it right now, that's okay."

For ten grades she had been little more than a speed bump in the Dan River Falls High social strata, but now she was suddenly worthwhile. Avery wondered if it was just because her father was the chief of police or because kids knew that Fletcher had asked for her. Either way, she was uneasy with the attention.

"Hey." Ellison squished into the five-inch space between Avery and another girl. Ellison wasn't big or outspoken, but she had a way of getting her message across and that's why Avery liked her.

"What's with the French homework?" Ellison asked, picking

a potato chip off Avery's lunch tray. "Is that what everyone's talking about?

Avery grabbed her tray and stood abruptly. "I've got to get to class."

• • •

"Fletcher...Fletcher..."

Fletcher shifted, realization dawning on him as his eyes adjusted to the darkness. He was at home, lying in his bed. The clock on his nightstand read 2:41, its red numbers glowing in the darkness. What woke him up?

"Fletcher..."

It was a low, throaty whisper, someone drawing out his name, holding the *R* for far too long.

Fletcher kicked off the covers and sat up, his gaze darting around his bedroom.

"Is someone here?"

"Fletcher..." It was like the voice was right beside him, lips whispering in his ear. He swore he could feel the breath on his face. He recognized the voice. His throat constricted; his lips trembled.

"Adam?"

Suddenly, there was a chorus of whispers. A low din, all of the words tangling together, voices all talking at once so he couldn't decipher one thread of conversation from the other. Where did Adam go?

"Adam?"

The whispers grew more insistent, and Fletcher swatted at his ear. "Shhhh!" he commanded.

The voices responded by getting louder, and a few discernable words broke through the murmuring: "Killer… Do it again… You could have saved him… Do it again… Killer."

He scrunched his eyes shut and pressed his hands over his ears. "Stop!"

"Fletcher!"

It was Adam; he was sure of it.

"Come on, man."

"Adam?" Fletcher could feel tears stinging his eyes. It was as if his saliva were thickening and sticking on Adam's name. *How could Adam be here? How could Adam be talking to him?*

"No." Fletcher's eyes flew open and he was staring at himself in the mirror, hands still clamped against his head. His cheeks were glossy with tears. "Why are you doing this to me?"

"Why are you doing this to me?" Adam's voice mocked. "Why are you doing this to me?"

NINE

Avery poked through the candy bowl on her father's desk. She unwrapped a Jolly Rancher, popped it in her mouth, and stared at the whiteboard in front of her. It usually drifted from office to office, filled with colorful scrawl and "notes to remember." It looked totally different now.

Avery knew what it was: a murder board. She also knew that somewhere on her father's desk was the murder book, a three-ringed binder that would grow fat with each new piece of evidence from Adam's murder—documents, photographs, witness statements. Her statement.

She wanted to look away, but she couldn't. The board fascinated her.

Scotch-taped to the upper left corner were smiling school portraits of both Adam and Fletcher with their names written underneath in red marker. The word "deceased" was scrawled in parentheses below Adam's name. A vague timeline ran across the top of the board, an imperfect black line hashed with slashes: *12 noon boys leave Adam's house; 13:03 arrive at Cascade Mountain*

Park, Lot B. A photocopy of a faded parking receipt was taped by the black hash mark, next to a long blank space. Someone had inserted a Post-it note and written, "Lime Kiln Trail (3.8 mi); no witness came forward/per vic: no one seen on trail."

Avery scanned the next few entries—"vic (FC) reported missing by mother M. Carroll, OFC KG and RH prelim search." Her stomach dropped. A handful of crime-scene photographs were arranged at the end of the timeline.

Most were of where they found the boys, but one showed Avery, eyes wide and bleached by the camera flash, as she knelt next to Fletcher, her hand looped with his. There was a smear of blood—Fletcher's blood—on the back of her hand. Avery's hand burned as though the blood were still there.

Then, in her mind, she saw her mother's body crumpled and pinned by the steering wheel. Her blood had begun to pool on the seat. It was so impossibly red that Avery had been mesmerized by its rich, jeweled hue. She never knew that one body could hold so much blood.

• • •

The interrogation room looked nothing like the ones Fletcher had seen on TV. It was small, and instead of two chairs and a table with handcuff loops, there were a long, wooden veneer desk, a dusty fake ficus, and an ugly couch that looked like it had come from someone's bachelor pad. The walls were made of those Styrofoam-looking cement tiles like in school, and the carpet was the same industrial gray as Fletcher had seen at every other business in town. He fingered his cup of water and wondered if they were going to use it to collect evidence, lifting his DNA or maybe a row of fingerprints from it. *But evidence for what?*

They have all that, he reminded himself. It all came flooding back in a hot blur: Chief Templeton leading a lady cop into his hospital room, her inking his hands, then rolling his fingertips, one by one, on a card. The woman had used gentle pressure, but just her fingers on his caused an explosion of pain, and the line of stitches on his right index finger had left a weird smudge.

What about the whispers?

He hadn't heard them since that night—well, not Adam. The whispers crept up on him every once in a while, muttering words he couldn't quite make out, clouded figures chattering just beyond the edge of his periphery. He pressed his fingertips to his temples. The mere thought of the voices sent a ripple of fear down his spine.

"Fletcher, sorry to keep you waiting."

Fletcher looked up nervously and dropped his hands into his lap.

The man was wearing a Men's Wearhouse suit that didn't quite fit right, with an American flag pin on the lapel of the jacket. A DRFPD badge hung on a chain around his neck.

"I'm Detective Malloy." His green eyes gave Fletcher a once-over, and he nodded at Fletcher's water. "I see Connie got you something to drink. Would you rather have a Coke or something?"

Fletcher shook his head. His grip tightened on the cup, his palm sweating. *Adam is dead.* Adam was dead, and he had barely escaped the woods with his life, and Detective Malloy wanted to know if he'd like a Coke.

"Can we just get this over with, please?" Fletcher's voice sounded small and the detective nodded.

"I can only imagine how hard this must be for you, losing your friend like that. And then we have to bring you through it over and over again." Malloy shrugged, his face apologetic. "I'm really sorry, son. It's procedure."

The word "son" stuck out of Malloy's sentence, and Fletcher almost wanted to laugh. Not even his father called him "son," unless he was talking to Fletcher's mother. Then it was "*your* son"—as in, "Your son has ruined everything again."

Malloy clicked open his ballpoint pen. "I know we've talked before and you've talked to Chief Templeton already. How you feeling, by the way?"

Fletcher instinctively touched the pads of his fingers to the bandage wrapped around his head. The stitches itched but didn't hurt. Everything else hurt. "I'm okay," he lied.

"So, the twelfth of September. It was a Saturday…"

Malloy didn't need to say the date or the day of the week. "That night" was all the description that would ever be needed. As Malloy talked, Fletcher's eyes felt heavy. His lips start to move as he recounted the story yet again.

"We were in Adam's room and kind of bored. We thought we'd go for a hike."

He remembered that Adam's mother had come in, carrying a basket full of clean, folded laundry. She had set to work pushing the neat bundles into Adam's drawers when he'd rolled his eyes and told her to get out.

Fletcher closed his eyes and remembered the shards of sunlight that came in through the blinds. The vision morphed into the mottled sunlight in the forest. The pine had smelled so fresh and strong.

They had hiked for a while—a couple hours, maybe more—and far enough in so the trees were thick and close together. He couldn't remember if they were still walking or if they had stopped. They must have stopped. Fletcher racked his mind to remember why. What stopped them?

He tried to force a picture of himself with Adam, back on the trail. Fletcher had seen them do that kind of thing on cop shows to lead a witness to remember a detail that would crack the case. If he could just imagine himself with Adam on the trail, maybe he could remember what had happened. But his mind refused to cooperate.

He flashed back to the two of them sitting in Adam's bedroom, then riding in his car, then at the trailhead. Detective Malloy started to whisper.

Fletcher blinked. "Excuse me?"

Malloy looked up from his notepad. "What?"

"I didn't hear what you said."

Malloy looked confused. "I didn't say anything."

Frustration mounted in Fletcher's gut. "Just now. You were whispering."

"No." Malloy drew out the word.

Was this some kind of cop game? A strategy to make a witness feel crazy until he ultimately confessed? *Confess what?* Fletcher wanted to scream. He swallowed hard. "I-I guess I heard something else."

The detective resumed his questioning. "You say you left Adam's house and—you were driving, correct?"

Fletcher nodded, distracted.

"Fletcher, son, are you okay?"

The first blow came out of nowhere, and his entire body vibrated with the impact. Even his teeth rattled. He wasn't sure if he was still standing or if he'd been knocked off his feet. He tried to look around but all he could see was the mosaic of pine needles on the ground, and then his vision clouded and everything went red. Sweat pricked at the back of his neck and someone was talking to him, trying to get his attention.

"Fletcher? Fletcher? Are you okay, son?" Malloy's beady eyes looked concerned, his bushy brows diving into a V.

Fletcher blinked, the slap of pain clearing immediately. He was in the conference room. He was safe. He rubbed his hands against his jeans, his clammy palms catching on the fabric. His heart was wailing against his chest.

"I'm sorry," he said, working to focus on Malloy. "I just—"

Malloy held up one hand and blew out a long, slow breath. "That's okay, son. We're going to find this guy. You're going to be okay."

• • •

There was no parking at Dana & Mo's. But there was *always* parking at Dana & Mo's, especially on Thursday nights when Avery and her father came in at six forty-five for mammoth slices of the Kitchen Sink, a pizza laced with more toppings than Avery could count, all blended together in one harmonious, delicious mess of cheese and grease.

This Thursday night though, the parking lot was packed with cars. Kids from Dan River Falls High streamed from the doors and congregated in circles, laughing.

"What is going on?" Avery wanted to know.

Her father leaned over the seat and fished something out from a mass of papers, handing Avery a single blue page.

"A fund-raiser?"

"You didn't get one? Some kids were by the station earlier this week dropping them off. Weren't they up around school?"

Avery nodded, knowing that she had seen the fliers posted. She just hadn't stopped to see what they were advertising.

A black-and white photo of Fletcher was centered on the page, with FUND-RAISER FOR FLETCHER CAROL! and MEDICAL BILLS ARE EXPENSIVE in bubble writing with little frown-y faces bordering the shot.

"You didn't know about it?" the chief asked.

"I guess I've been a little distracted at school. Besides"—Avery pointed at FLETCHER CAROL—"this was obviously put on by Fletch's closest friends. The ones who don't even know how to spell his last name."

"Be nice. It's good that his peers are doing something for the Carrolls. They're going to need a lot of support to get through this."

She nodded. "I guess. I'm glad people are actually coming together for a good cause. It just sucks that this is what it takes for Fletch to get some recognition. I don't think anyone even noticed him before."

Avery thumbed at something on the window, not wanting to

look at her father, not wanting to think about Fletcher and all the kids inside who were pretending like he was their friend. The same thing had happened after her mother died. The kids who came around just wanted a firsthand account of the story, so they pretended they wanted to be there for Avery, pretended they had ever paid her any attention before. Then, once the story was no longer interesting and Avery wasn't getting back to "normal," they started to avoid her. She wondered if they would do the same thing to Fletcher.

"In that case, we'll get two Kitchen Sinks apiece," her dad said.

• • •

The news was officially out: Fletcher had narrowly escaped a savage murderer, but Adam hadn't been so lucky. Bouquets had poured into the Dan River Falls Community Hospital with notes calling Fletcher "a survivor" and "a miracle." The same floral arrangements were delivered to the Templeton house with deepest sympathies. And Avery was deemed a hero for finding Fletcher.

The tension in town was palpable. A citywide curfew was issued for anyone under eighteen, which meant that at 9:00 p.m., the streets were completely empty even though the sky was barely dark.

The news seemed to run on every channel, a twenty-four-hour loop of local news anchors looking stern and talking in serious tones while a news ticker ran underneath them with sensationalist headlines like "Terror Rocks Bedroom Community." Avery didn't know what a "bedroom community" was, nor that she had been living in one, until the incident. That's what everyone was calling it, "the incident." And everyone was talking about it.

Chief Templeton clicked off the television and ran a hand over his eyes. "Want to watch a movie?"

Avery looked over her shoulder at him from where she lay on the living-room floor. "You going to stay awake past the credits?"

Even in the dim light, she could see the hint of a smile on her dad's face. "Probably not."

"It's not even eight o'clock. Go to bed, old man."

"What are you going to do?"

"Burn down the house. What do you think?" She rolled onto her back and put her bare feet on the edge of the couch. "I might go for a bike ride."

The chief nudged Avery's feet. "Nope. Curfew."

"Dad, it's a bike—" She stopped, remembering that the curfew was for the entire city, not a grounding just for her. Not that she ever did anything to get grounded. "Forgot. Maybe I'll knit."

Her father stood up and yawned. "You don't know how to knit," he said as he trudged down the hall toward his bedroom.

"Then I guess it's back to burning the house down," Avery yelled at his back.

By nine fifteen, all her homework was done. Every album had been listened to, every website perused. Avery could hear her father's plaintive snores from down the hall. She had slept with her door cracked open ever since her mother died. The sound of her father snoring was annoying but proved he was alive, which comforted her.

She glanced around her room at the piles of what her father affectionately called "crap." Technically, she could clean her room but that sounded about as appealing as a lifelong algebra class, so she pulled a book from her bookshelf and curled up in her bed. She hadn't finished the first page before she heard the *pip-pip-pip* of something hitting her window. She paused, then immediately dismissed it.

Second floor. The chief of police's house. No one would be dumb enough to tap on the window, not with the whole town on edge. She glanced down at her open book again, relishing the silence as she started to read.

Pip-pip-pip.

It was back. A definite *pip*! Something hitting her window.

An electric zing of panic shot through her.

She *had* heard something.

Avery clicked off her bedroom lights and crept to the wall, crouching in a modified crab walk, her eyes straining to see over the sill with all of the flowers she had received, accompanied by mushy letters of praise and tokens of thanks from people she'd never met. She sucked in a shaky breath and glanced out the window, thinking one of those strangers had come for her. Or maybe the same person who had come for Adam and Fletcher.

The *pip-pip-pip* came again.

"Avery!"

It was half call, half whisper. Avery threw open the window. "Fletcher?"

He was standing on her driveway, half bathed in yellow streetlight, the bandages on his head and arms standing out stark white against the blue-black night.

"What are you doing?" she whispered.

"Come down."

She looked over her shoulder, then back at Fletcher. "My dad's asleep. He'll flip."

Fletcher looked down at his hands. Nearly every finger was bandaged or splinted—most of them both.

"Hold on."

She tiptoed past her father's room and slipped the lock on the back door—the only one in the entire house that didn't squeak—then walked down the driveway to Fletcher.

"You're out of the hospital." It was obvious, so a stupid remark, but Fletcher smiled anyway.

"Yeah, they released me this morning."

"And you decided the best thing for your recovery was a midnight walk over to my place?"

Fletcher snorted. "It's barely ten and 'your place' is around the corner. Not exactly a cross-country trek, Ave."

Ave. No one had called her Ave in at least a year.

"So?" Avery raised her eyebrows.

"I just had to get out of the house. My mom was hovering, staring at me. I'd fall asleep with her watching me, and when I'd wake up, she'd still be watching me."

"Creepy."

"Yeah, I guess she thinks this dude is going to come to finish me off or something." He shuddered.

Avery was quiet for a moment, and then she asked, "Do you remember who did this to you?"

His lips pursed and his forehead wrinkled. She could tell that he was searching for a word or a memory.

Fletcher shook his head. "I don't remember anything."

They walked to the end of the block in companionable silence, then continued toward the baseball diamond. Finally, Fletcher cleared his throat.

"Did you get the flowers?"

"I got tons of flowers. I don't know why though. I didn't do anything."

"No. From me. I-I sent you flowers. You know, just to say thanks." Even in the darkness she could see that he was blushing, a fierce red that went up to his ears. "I mean, it's no big deal. Not you finding me, the flowers. The flowers—they are not a big deal. You know, just to say thanks."

"There were a couple of bunches on the front steps when we got home tonight. To be honest, I hadn't read the cards yet."

"That's cool."

There was another beat of awkward quiet, just the sound of their shoes crunching the dirt over the diamond.

"Remember at the hospital when I asked you what you think happens when we die?"

Avery stopped, the breath snatched from her chest. "Yeah."

"I can't stop thinking about it. I try not to, but…do you think people go somewhere immediately? Or do they—do they maybe hang around? Unfinished business and all that."

Avery had considered the same question every day, what felt like every moment, for months after her mother died. She pored over texts and the Bible and did Internet searches on every myth and legend and belief possible. Not one gave her a solid answer. Not one gave her enough satisfaction to feel peace, to feel whole again.

She shrugged.

Fletch seemed to drop the subject and smiled, rolling his head back to look at the sky. "It's kind of nice out here right now. No one but us, you know?"

Avery huffed a laugh. "Don't tell me you're already getting tired of your adoring fans."

A stitch of pain crossed Fletcher's face and Avery felt guilty. "I didn't mean that—"

"No"—Fletcher shrugged her off—"I know it's weird. People act like I'm some kind of hero because I survived."

"Well, you escaped. And because of that, we were able to find Adam."

He shook his head. "Fat lot of good that did."

"But…you are alive. Which means there is a better chance the police can catch this guy. You know, because you're a witness and stuff."

Fletcher loosened a rock with the toe of his sneaker, then picked it up, rolling it in the palm of his "good" hand. "Did I already say, 'Fat lot of good that did'? I can't remember worth shit."

"It'll come back," Avery said, awkwardly patting his elbow. She had never really *touched* Fletcher before. Or any boy, for that matter. They were casual friends who greeted each other with a head nod, and that was it.

Fletcher asked, "People treated you different after your mom died, right?"

Avery pinched her lips together and looked off in the distance. "Well, yeah. I mean, at first it was, 'I'm so sorry,' and after a while it was, 'Aren't you over that yet?'" There was an edge of anger in her voice.

"When did people start treating you normally again?"

Avery picked up her own rock, palmed it, then sent it on a line drive past the pitcher's mound. "They didn't. The way they treated me became the new normal."

"People never paid any attention to me before all this happened, but I think that was better." He dropped his rock. It rolled over his bandaged fingers and plunked onto the ground at his feet. "I think being ignored is better than everyone watching me. I—"

"Wait." Avery reached out for Fletcher instinctively, her hand circling his wrist.

There was a light rustling behind them.

A prickle of nerves shot down her spine. "Did you hear that?" She yanked him to the ground. "There's someone here."

Avery knew every covert tactic, thanks to her father's love of spy movies, but she was sure the thundering beat of her heart would give away their location at the edge of the baseball diamond. Her heart only thumped harder when the bushes across from them shook and a figure stepped out. They could see it was a person from the glow of streetlights, but that was it.

The person swiped something against a tree trunk. A flame caught on the tip of the match, which glowed fluorescent orange, illuminating the hard angles of the man's face. His thin lips were bared, and he held a cigarette between his yellowed teeth.

"What do we have here?" The guy jutted his chin toward Avery and Fletcher, and then took a long drag from his cigarette. He squinted, cupping his hand over his eyes as if there was glare from the sun. Then he rolled back on his heels, satisfied.

"Huh! You that kid on the news? The one that got all beat up. The little bitch that ran away. Is this your little girlfriend, faggot?"

The guy shifted. His cheeks were pockmarked and still spotted with acne. His hair was greasy and plastered hard against his forehead.

"Jimmy Jerold?" Avery asked.

Jimmy Jerold was the stuff that nightmares were made of—the high-school dropout who still hung around, selling pot and pills in the school parking lot. He was always getting arrested. His two nicotine-stained fingers gripped his cigarette, and he blew out a long, white pouf of smoke.

"Your little girlfriend knows me."

Avery could see Fletcher stiffen beside her. He took a small step forward toward Jimmy, effectively stepping in front of Avery. "Dude, we were just talking," Fletcher said, his voice calm. "We're cool."

Jimmy moved like a flash and was nearly nose to nose with Fletcher. "We ain't cool, *dude*."

TEN

Avery's stomach plummeted as the glare of the streetlight caught the blade of Jimmy's knife pressed against Fletcher's neck. Fletcher was on his tiptoes, with Jimmy gripping a fistful of his shirt.

"Leave him alone, Jimmy!"

"This pitiful son of a bitch? Maybe I should gut him. Finish him off. You were supposed to die out there, you know. You and your little bitch boyfriend." Jimmy blew a huff of smoke into Fletcher's face, and his lips thinned as he grinned sadistically.

Fletcher just stared straight ahead as if he wasn't seeing Jimmy.

"Fletch—" she started.

Blue-and-white lights cut through the darkness and Jimmy let go of Fletcher's shirt, shoving him backward. Avery grabbed Fletcher's arm to support him, and they both started to run. Avery could hear his breath straining as he kept pace with her, his weight balanced against her shoulder until her house came into view. They doubled over in her driveway.

Adrenaline crashed through Avery's system and she blinked, her throat tightening. "Oh my God, that guy is a psychopath." She could feel tears forming. "I'm so sorry, Fletcher."

Fletcher stood in front of her, his eyes hard and dark. "He said I was supposed to die out there." His voice was little more than a hoarse whisper. "What do you think—"

Avery stepped backward, her lower lip trembling. "Fletcher." She gestured at his chest, unable to push the words past her lips.

He looked to where she was pointing. There was a starburst of wrinkles on the cotton where Jimmy's fist had been. In the center, like the stamen of some hideous flower, was a smear of blood. Fletcher didn't raise his head again before turning on his heel and walking into the night.

• • •

I shoulda killed him. I shoulda killed him. The words swirled around in his head. The faster he walked, the more the night air broke over his face. His hands were fisted so tightly that his fingernails dug into his palms.

The metallic waft of the blood on his shirt assaulted him, and he felt something noxious roiling in his gut. That smell…

A thick, dense forest of pine trees surrounded him. Somewhere, a river flowed. He could hear it. He should have been able to smell it too—the fresh, mossy scent of the water, let alone the heady, sharp scent of the pine needles that cushioned his step. But the dull, metallic stench of the blood overtook all of his senses.

"Adam?" Fletcher called. There was no response. His voice came out shaky and weak. "Adam, dude, where are you?"

There was a rustle from somewhere behind Fletcher. It wasn't big enough to be a bear, but was too large to be a squirrel. It was like his body knew the sound before his mind did. He tensed. Every inch of his body sensed danger in the most primitive way. Sweat burned his eyes and poured down the back of his shirt.

It was coming for him. He needed to run. He needed to get away.

A branch shook. A twig snapped. Someone took another step through the foliage. But Fletcher was frozen. It was as if he had been turned into a statue. He thought his head was going to explode or his heart would blow through his chest. He wanted to growl, to roar, to make himself big and terrifying and impassable.

"Adam…" His voice was a mere whisper now, strained with tears and terror. "God, Adam. Man, where the fuck are you?"

Then the smell of blood grew stronger. He looked down. Fresh droplets fanned across the toes of his sneakers. Another drop fell and a fresh wave of nausea crashed over him. He looked up, trying to locate where the drop came from. Branches stretched above him, but that was all. He looked down at his shoes again as another drop fell at the edge of his vision, burning a trail down his cheek.

Fletcher retched. Through his daze, he had made it home. Kneeling in front of the toilet, he felt his whole body convulse. He was pretty sure he'd already thrown up every bit of food he'd ever eaten in his life.

"Fletch, honey, is that you?"

His mother clicked on the bathroom light, and Fletcher pinched his eyes shut at the harsh fluorescent glare. She put her hand on his back, then immediately pulled it away. "You're sweating. Honey, are you sick? Do you have a fever?"

Fletcher flushed the toilet as his mother arranged a wet washcloth on the back of his neck.

"Do you need more pain medication? Or is the pain medication making you sick?"

His head was still swimming with images of Jimmy. He pushed the pads of his fingers against his temples and rubbed small circles, trying to quell his headache.

"I don't know, Mom. The pain meds make me feel crazy." He shrugged and pushed himself up from the bathroom floor. "I think I'm okay though. Maybe it was just something I ate." He gave his mother a quick peck on the cheek. "Go back to sleep. Sorry I woke you."

He started down the hall, but his mother stopped him. "Fletcher, if there was something wrong—something wrong again—you would tell me, right?" Her smile was weak but her eyes were hopeful. "We can talk about things, you know."

Anger swelled in his chest and his headache thumped like a bass drum. "I'm fine, Ma. It's probably just something I ate. I'm going back to sleep." He pushed the washcloth back into her hand, strode into his room, and shut the door.

• • •

Avery snuck back into her house completely undetected. If she were a normal teenager, this would be a triumph, but she was Avery Templeton, daughter of the chief of police and lifelong do-gooder, so it troubled her that her father's snores didn't shift in the slightest.

So did what had just happened with Jimmy Jerold.

She tried to scrunch her eyes shut and fall asleep counting sheep or listening to music on her iPhone, but with the tension thrumming through her body, every sheep or song dissolved into the terrifying snarl on Jimmy Jerold's face...and the expressionless look on Fletcher's. She wasn't sure which disturbed her more—the fact that she likely had stood toe-to-toe with Adam's killer or the stony, unaffected way her friend had reacted. A line she had read in class swam in the back of her mind:

"...Sometimes, in an effort to protect itself, the brain turns off certain functions, particularly in the light of trauma or a trigger."

Avery started to breathe harder. Fletcher might not remember that Jimmy was there on the hike that day, but maybe his brain did. Maybe his body did but he had been frozen in fear.

She sat bolt upright and made a beeline for her father's bed.

"Dad," she whispered, gently poking his shoulder. "Dad."

It took little more than a heavy breath to wake her father, who was on his feet in the amount of time it took for most people to blink. Instinctively he reached for the gun belt but stopped when he thunked into Avery.

"Avery? Is everything okay? Are you okay?"

She nodded, sitting on the edge of his bed. "Maybe. Yeah, I mean, not really." She gnawed her bottom lip. "Dad, Fletcher came by. He and I snuck out tonight."

Her father sucked in a heavy breath. One eyebrow was arched and Avery could tell that he was pressing his lips so as not to interrupt her story. But he was not happy.

"I'm sorry. I'm really, really sorry."

"Avery, you broke a house rule and you broke a city law. Is this you just coming clean?"

"No, Dad, that's not the point."

"No, Avery, I think that very much is the point."

Avery groaned. "Dad! Just listen to me. I'm sorry about sneaking out and you can punish me, but something happened."

Suddenly, Chief Templeton's dad face was replaced by his cop face: hard, penetrating eyes, slightly cocked head. "Tell me."

"We weren't doing anything. Fletcher had been cooped up and just needed to get out of the house so he came by here. We walked out to the old diamond—"

The chief pinched the bridge of his nose. "The point, sweetheart."

"We ran into Jimmy Jerold." Avery was more terrified than she had been when Jimmy was actually in front of her. "He was watching us. He came out of the bushes and started calling Fletch a faggot."

"I'm sorry, Avy, but—"

"Listen! He held Fletcher up by his shirt, like this"—Avery demonstrated on her own nightshirt—"and he told Fletcher that he should have died. Dad, he said that Fletcher was supposed to die in the woods too."

Chief Templeton straightened. "Are you sure? That's exactly what he said?"

Avery nodded. "And something else. There was a car. When it drove by, Jimmy let go of Fletch and we took off running. But when we got back here, there was blood on Fletcher's shirt. Right where Jimmy had grabbed him. Dad, Jimmy Jerold had blood on his hands. He came out of the bushes at the edge of the forest. I think maybe he killed Adam."

ELEVEN

Fletcher knew everyone was going to stare at him. He figured some would point and there would be whispers, but he never expected the greeting he got on campus the next day. Two girls smiled at him. A jock named Biff or Bill or Brian fist-bumped him. Mrs. Taylor hunched over his desk in biology, telling him, "If at any time you need a break or something gets too much for you, just raise your hand and go straight to the nurse. She'll let you lie down."

He could feel his cheeks burning and the sweat turning his palms slick as he gripped the sides of his desk. Mrs. Taylor was so close. He could taste the bitter alcohol in her rose-scented perfume. Fletcher didn't know where to look. If he looked at her eyes, he would see her pity. He was too embarrassed to look at the soft crest of her ample cleavage as she leaned over to speak with him, so he stared at the back of Ford Winston's head, at the gel-covered spikes of black hair cutting across his bone-white scalp.

The cops had picked up Jimmy Jerold sometime last night—or maybe sometime this morning. Fletcher had slept through his alarm and was late to homeroom, but the news had already torn through the entire school: Jimmy Jerold and Fletcher had a run-in, and Jimmy talked about that day in the woods. Jimmy killed Adam and he was going to kill Fletcher too.

Fletcher shifted in his seat, the weight of his classmates' stares heavy on him. Maria Gray, perfect and perky in her tight jeans and shrink-wrapped T-shirt, smiled at him, batting her eyes. When Mrs. Taylor walked away, Maria leaned in, casually draping one slim, caramel-colored arm across his desk.

"So is it true? Jimmy Jerold came back for you last night and you escaped again?"

Fletcher blinked. "Uh…"

Maria grabbed his hand, her thumb stroking the back of his. "I didn't know you were so brave," she purred, "or so strong."

Fletcher shifted. Maria Gray had never spoken to him before. Ever. She'd bump into him and say nothing, not even an apology. And suddenly, she was stroking Fletcher's hand like a kitten and studying his face with her wide, cocoa-brown eyes.

"I-I've—" he stuttered, and then raised the hand that Maria was holding. Mrs. Taylor gave him a nod that he was excused.

"Hey, Fletch, way to go, man." Ford clapped Fletcher on the back as he gathered up his backpack.

"Glad you're safe," a female voice said.

"You're a hero, man. You caught Adam's killer."

There was a smattering of applause and agreement as Fletcher stood, but he stared at his shoes as he made his way out of the classroom. The stitches underneath the bandage on his forehead were starting to throb, and the edges of his peripheral vision were starting to fog and go black.

The last thing he saw before he left the room was the empty seat. It was right at the front of the class, first row for the star student. It was Adam's desk.

• • •

Fletcher and Adam's case was only getting bigger, and so was the attention focused on Avery in the school hallway. She tried to shrink into her black hoodie, hoping to draw attention away from herself.

"So, is it true that you were out with Fletcher last night?"

Avery wasn't even sure who asked the question because when she looked around, everyone was facing her, every kid waiting for her to speak.

"I can't really talk about it," Avery said, turning on her heel in time to see two girls—seniors, probably—pointing and staring at her with narrowed eyes.

"Hey," one of the girls said. "Are you Avery?"

The girl stood a whole head taller than Avery and had boobs that generously filled her black-and-red T-shirt. Avery shrank deeper into her sweatshirt, painfully aware that she had the body of a twelve-year-old boy.

"Yeah. Who are you?"

Avery wasn't ready for the hands on her shoulders or the heaving push that knocked her off her feet and into the crowd that had assembled behind her. The girl in the tank top got in Avery's face, her eyes sharp and dark, her red-lipsticked mouth pulled into a hideous snarl.

Avery instinctively put her hands up, defending her face, but the girl didn't shove her again.

"You got my boyfriend put in jail, you little bitch! Jimmy wasn't even in the woods that night!"

"I-I didn't—" Someone pushed Avery forward, trying to stand her upright. Someone else yelled behind her, "Get away from her, Rachel! Your boyfriend is a murderer!"

"Leave her alone!" someone else screeched before the din of voices blurred into one and Avery rode the crowd, being shoved backward, then forward. She howled when someone grabbed her hair, tugging until her scalp burned. Someone else pulled on her sweatshirt, and when she looked to see who it was, she only got punched in the nose. Arms flew, fingers clawed, and you couldn't tell who was fighting whom. It was an all-out melee in the junior hallway of Dan River Falls High, and Avery Templeton was in the middle of it.

"Stop! Stop!"

The shrill sound of a whistle cut through the yelling, and there was a brief pause in the fight—long enough for Avery to slip through the crowd and press her shoulders against the wall, doing her best to make herself flat and invisible.

"Come on!"

Principal Corben was suddenly in the middle of everything, pushing kids apart. Coach Krail and Mr. Parsons stepped in too, screaming something about suspension.

The crowd quickly thinned. Avery breathed hard, the panic humming through her body. Fevered images slashed through her mind at nauseating speeds: the crushed car at the edge of the woods. The spinning lights from the police cruisers. The sound of the officers yelling, warning her to stay back. The blood. Her mother's blood.

"Avery?" Principal Corben appeared in front of her. "You're bleeding. Let's get you to the nurse's office."

Avery nodded numbly and followed him. "What happened here, Ms. Templeton?"

Her nerves buzzed like bees in her head. "I really don't know. Someone—I guess Jimmy Jerold's girlfriend—shoved me. She thinks I put Jimmy in jail." Avery felt briefly guilty, as though she had been the one to do something wrong. But then she thought of Jimmy Jerold and the blade of that knife resting against Fletcher's skin. The anger crashed over her. "Jimmy deserves to go to jail."

• • •

It was cool and dark in the nurse's office. Nurse Katie was a heavyset older woman who looked like a grandmother on a greeting card. She smiled at Fletcher, directed him to a cot, and handed him a blanket.

"Your parents didn't register any pain medication with me. Would you like me to call home for you?"

"My mom."

"What's that now?"

Fletcher bit his bottom lip, then touched the bandage on his head. It was becoming almost a security thing, touching the bandage as if to make sure that everything that had happened to him, to Adam, had been real and not some sick and twisted dream.

"My dad's gone. It's just my mom. And no, I don't need any pain medication."

Nurse Katie stood at the edge of the bed, wringing her hands. Fletcher could tell that she wanted to pat him—his leg or his shoulder. She looked like a patter, one of those old-school ladies who liked to hug and pinch cheeks and pat.

"You're very brave," she said finally. "What happened to Adam was tragic, but bless God, you escaped. Very frightening that something like that could happen in a little town like ours."

Fletcher didn't know how he was supposed to respond. Say thank you? Agree? He said nothing but turned onto his side and stared at the wall, waiting until he heard the squeak of Nurse Katie's shoes on the linoleum.

He was tired but he couldn't rest. He had barely slept last night, his eyes opening every hour or so as foggy dreams turned into lucid ones, ones where he was in the forest and rage was consuming him as he struck out, bone thwacking against bone. Sometimes he saw Adam in his dream; other times his father towered over him. Each time he awoke, he was sweating and the sheets were twisted around his legs. Each time he could faintly smell the trailing scent of pine intermixed with the acrid smell of blood.

Then the murmurings would start again.

Hushed. Wordless. Like a staticky chorus. Fletcher was motionless in the darkness, straining to decipher the whispers over the beating of his heart. Then he heard footsteps. Breathing.

The man who killed Adam is back. Fletcher could feel him hiding in the shadows of his bedroom. Or maybe he was waiting outside the door. Fletcher started to pace his house, searching, daring to sneak glances through the windows, both sure and not sure of what he would see. Would he look into the eyes of a killer lurking there or his own reflection?

He had never found any intruders.

A triangle of fluorescent light cut into the darkened nurse's office, and Fletcher could hear low voices. Both were female. He recognized one as Nurse Katie's.

"You just go on in there and lie down, hon. And keep that ice pack over your nose. Doesn't look too bad, but it could swell. Your father is on his way."

He could hear the other student settle on the bed across from him, the plasticky vinyl groaning as the kid got comfortable. He heard the unmistakable crunch of an instant cold pack—he had been covered in them in the hospital. Fletcher cut his eyes over his shoulder.

"Avery?"

Half her face was covered by the ice pack and her hair looked like she had brushed it with a blender, but it was definitely Avery Templeton.

She turned her head toward him. "Hey, Fletcher."

Fletcher sat up. "What happened to you?"

Avery stared at the ceiling again, moving the ice pack aside and touching the bridge of her nose gingerly. She winced and pressed the ice pack back against her face.

"Some senior happened to me. She said Jimmy was in jail and that he was innocent, and somehow the whole thing was all my fault."

"Then she slugged you?"

Avery shrugged. "Someone did. It was like a riot."

Fletcher let out something between a sigh and a laugh. "A riot? That kind of stuff doesn't happen here."

"Neither do murders."

There was a moment of awkward silence. Fletcher's mind spun, thinking of something to say. But Avery started talking.

"Do you think he told anyone?"

"Who? Jimmy?"

Avery shifted, the ice pack crinkling as she did. "Yeah. Do you think he told anyone what he did to…"—her voice dropped to a choked, low whisper—"what he did to you guys?"

Now Fletcher lay back and stared at the pockmarked ceiling above him. "I-I don't know. If you kill someone, who would you tell?"

He could hear the release of Avery's breath in the darkness. "I don't know."

"I don't think a guy who would kill someone could have any friends."

"Two people," Avery said.

"What?"

"He tried to kill two people, Fletch. He killed Adam and he meant to kill you."

Fletcher thought of Jimmy Jerold, of the way he'd bitten off his words when he had Fletcher by the shirtfront, little flecks of spittle flying from the corners of his mouth. He could still feel the hate that had rolled off Jimmy and the look of his cold, black eyes.

Was he there that day?

Calling up the memories, Fletcher felt the pain in his skull intensify and he started to salivate, certain he was going to throw up. He swallowed back bile and tried to remember Jimmy's boots stomping across the forest clearing, the sound they made when they crunched over curls of bark and broken leaves. But the memory always disintegrated like an old-fashioned film catching fire—little spots of black marring the images here and there, until the spots ran together and the whole picture disappeared.

Fletcher heard Adam's voice though, loud and distinctive: *Hey— hey, man. What the—what the fuck do you think you're doing?*

• • •

Fletcher's house was dark when he let himself in. It was still light outside—school had only let out a few hours ago—but all the curtains were drawn, casting eerie shadows. His mother said she was protecting the furniture from fading in the summer sun, but the curtains didn't open in winter either.

He rummaged through the fridge for something to eat and a Coke, then dropped his sweatshirt and backpack on his bedroom floor before flopping down on the bed. His head had been throbbing since he saw Avery in the nurse's office. The idea that someone had slugged her needled at him. Why would someone attack Avery? She had nothing to do with the situation at all.

They didn't find me, Avery. You did.

His own voice floated back to him, and his mind returned to the forest once more. He blinked in the semidarkness, smelling that fresh-turned earth as Avery slid toward him.

His stomach quivered. Was he back? The guy who did this to him—to

Adam? Fletcher swore he could hear everything—the pat, pat, pat of the fire ant's footsteps. The crackling sound tree bark made as it started to dry and curl. The short, ragged breaths of someone closing in on him.

He knew he should move, but everything hurt. If the guy was coming back, Fletcher really hoped he would finish him off this time, just like he did Adam.

And then he saw Avery.

Not a savior. Not an angel. Just a girl. Her brown hair was pulled into a ponytail. She leaned in to him, and Fletcher could smell her, something faint and fruity—coconut or lime...

Fletcher sat bolt upright on the bed.

...Fletcher really hoped he would finish him off this time, just like he did Adam.

"Oh my God." His hand flew to the bandage, to the soft ache of the stitches and the cut underneath. "I knew Adam was dead."

Dread spread through him. He remembered. His brain had locked up memories and was leaking them out little by little. He pressed the pads of his fingers against his eyes. "Remember, God damn it. Remember something."

But all he could see was darkness. He flopped back on his bed, his body suddenly a thousand pounds of lead.

"Just fucking remember *something*."

TWELVE

It wasn't Avery's father who picked her up. It was Deputy Fenster—or Karen, to Avery. She arrived in her squad car and crisp black uniform, her white-blond hair tucked into a bun that sat just above her collar. Avery knew that hair above the collar was a standard part of the Dan River Falls Police Department's uniform, along with clean, clipped nails and manicured facial hair. She always thought it was funny that facial hair should be "manicured," and as a kid she imagined men walking around with moustaches and beards painted in nail-polish colors, like Fusion Pink or Ravishing Red.

"That's a heck of a shiner you've got, kid."

Karen had been a part of Avery's life for as long as she could remember, but ever since her mother died, the deputy was dispatched—or came on her own—whenever Avery needed something her father couldn't deal with. She showed up for back-to-school shopping and taught Avery how to French-braid her own hair. She drove Avery to buy new bras and tampons. But driving Avery home from a fight was a first.

Avery tugged on her seat belt. "What did my dad say?"

"He was worried about you," Karen said, her eyes flicking from the road for a beat.

Avery must have looked panicked because Karen slowed the car for a mile or two and went back to looking straight ahead. Ever since her mother's accident, Avery had been terrified of anyone who dared to take her eye off the road.

"He wanted to pick you up himself but he was prepping for the press conference."

"You don't have to do that, Karen."

Karen made a smooth turn off the highway. "Do what?"

"Reassure me that my father loves me."

Karen raised her eyebrows and her lips quirked up into a half smile. "You're too smart for your own good, Avery. He'll probably be home in an hour or so. The conference is supposed to go live at three."

Avery nodded, blowing out a long sigh. "Good. That'll give me enough time to get a helmet and one of Dad's bulletproof vests."

"Honey, are you scared? You're not in any danger."

"I will be when that press conference runs." She pointed to her blackened eye when Karen frowned. "This? A thank-you gift from Jimmy Jerold's girlfriend. She knows I was the one who told Dad what he said and got him arrested." She huffed something like a laugh. "She's dating a killer and *I* get the black eye."

Karen slowed down the car as they pulled onto Avery's street. "Oh, Avery, we let Jimmy Jerold go."

Now it was Avery's turn to frown. "What? Why? Didn't you

hear what he said to Fletcher? Even if he denied it, there are two witnesses. Two very reliable witnesses. And the blood. Why did they let him go?"

Karen pulled into the driveway and pushed the cruiser into park. "Jimmy had an airtight alibi."

"He had blood on his shirt, Karen. Human blood!"

She cocked her head, a chunk of hair falling from her bun. "How do you know the blood was human?"

Avery's stomach dropped. "I—it just—wasn't it Adam's? Or Fletcher's?"

"Fletcher's T-shirt is at the lab right now. They're running tests, but all we know is that it's blood. Jimmy handed over his clothes too, and those are being tested."

Avery felt bile itch in her throat, and for the first time since the incident, she felt real fear. "So whoever did this could still be out there?"

"It's beginning to look that way," Karen said, apology withering her voice.

Avery looked out the window. This was her town: the Buy Rite, the gas station, the Buzz Biz, her elementary school. She had biked through every parking lot, hung out at every strip-mall yogurt shop. It was a town where everyone knew everyone else and she should have felt comfortable, but now it was tainted. Behind the pleasant facade, evil lurked. Someone had killed once and was probably waiting to kill again. Was anyone safe?

A tremble of fear, cold like the breath of a ghost, snaked through her body.

"Do you want me to stay with you until your dad comes home?" Karen asked as Avery got out of the car.

Avery glanced at the "safety" light on in the living room and back at Karen. Fear still pricked at the base of her spine, but she shook her head. "I'll be fine."

Nothing in the house is going to get me, she reassured herself.

Avery waved at Karen, then hurried to the front door and sunk her key in the lock.

"Nothing is going to get me," she repeated out loud.

The house was exactly the way Avery and her dad had left it that morning—blinds partially drawn, unread newspaper still rubber-banded on the dining table, her father's glasses perched on top as though he were about to read but had gotten distracted. But something inside felt off.

Gooseflesh rippled the skin on her arms and neck as Avery dropped her backpack. Her ears pricked, waiting for the squeak of a shoe, a rustle of clothing, a door being closed too carefully.

The lace curtain over the sink fluttered with a gust of wind, and Avery slammed the window shut. She couldn't remember ever opening or closing that window. Neither she nor her father ever touched it. She scrutinized it. The window was small, but still large enough that someone Avery's size, or even a bit larger, could slide right through. She inched it open again and brushed her palm against the screen. It seemed to be secured, but that didn't mean anything. Had her father opened the window?

The tiny, empty vase that usually sat on the windowsill was knocked over, shattered blue glass in the sink.

Did someone crawl through?

Blood rushed through Avery's ears.

It was the wind, she scolded herself. *The wind blew the vase over.*

But who had opened the window?

"Hello?" Avery called—then immediately slapped her palm against her forehead. "Oh my God, I'm like every stupid girl in a horror movie. Hello," she sang out again, "I'm a lonely, unarmed girl. If you're here to kill me, please start your chain saw!" She laughed off the tension in her muscles, but she didn't feel any better. Jimmy Jerold had been freed. Someone *was* still out there.

She clicked on every downstairs light, even though it was the middle of the afternoon, and turned on the television, relishing the obnoxiously loud commercial for some blue kid's drink. Once it ended, the news popped on. The two anchors were coifed and positioned to look stiff and serious as a thunder of music rolled in the background.

"And now we go to Chief Effron Templeton at the Dan River Falls Police Department with the latest on the homicide in the Cascade Mountain area and the daring escape of one of the young victims."

The camera panned the American flags in front of the police department and the Dan River Falls Police sign before settling on her father. He looked stern faced behind a podium, flanked by an information officer and Officer Blount.

The chief introduced the incident, running quickly over the details. Avery could practically give the speech with him, she'd heard it so many times. Then he went on.

"It is true that we had a suspect in custody."

The news reporters and community members in the audience murmured their interest.

"That gentleman had an alibi and is no longer considered a suspect or person of interest in this case. Once again, all of our officers are working around the clock to find Adam Marshall's killer and bring him to justice. But we implore you, the community, to stay in contact with us. If you hear anything or may have seen anything, even if it seemed unimportant, please bring it to our attention. Parents, you may have heard your kids talking about a run-in with someone or possibly some trouble at school. Let us know. Again, we are doing everything we can to find the person or persons responsible—"

"Chief Templeton!" A woman in a maroon suit shoved her hand in the air. "Would you consider the people of Dan River Falls in any danger? There is, after all, a killer on the loose, and you said yourself the police department has virtually no leads."

Avery watched her father stiffen before sliding right back into his controlled public persona.

"We believe that this was an isolated incident and that the people of this community are in no imminent danger. That being said, always be aware and alert. Lock your doors. Act in a safe manner. And with all due respect, ma'am, I didn't say that the police department was without leads. By clearing our suspect, we're one person closer to the perpetrator. That is all."

The reporters broke into a frenzy like sharks circling their prey. Avery could almost hear their snapping jaws as they clamored to get their questions answered before her father disappeared into the police station.

When the woman in maroon ducked out of the frame, Avery sucked in a shocked breath.

Fletcher was at the press conference.

He was on the periphery of the swarm, the bandage on his head half hidden by a baseball hat pulled low and the yellowing bruises on his face shaded by the bill of his cap.

While everyone around him hummed with excitement at the chief's comments, Fletcher just stood there. And as the camera panned out, he threw his leg over his bike and rode away.

• • •

Fletcher's heart pounded like a kettledrum as he rode his bike, and he made a mental note to google if stress could give a kid a heart attack. *That's what it was, right? Stress?* He didn't want to admit that he was scared by the vision he kept having.

In it, the sun shone through the redwoods, and he and Adam were alone. Fletcher could feel something take over his body, making his muscles stiffen and hum. He watched his own hands curl into fists. He could feel his arm lift, but he couldn't control it. He couldn't control the recoil or the punch. As the vision grew clearer, he saw each punch as it landed on Adam. *Smack!* But he never saw more because he always started panting, his arms aching.

Normalcy. That's what he craved. A day where every moment was linked to the next with clarity, where every moment was actually lived, not under cover of blackness or accompanied by the scraping ache in his head.

He rode down the main road. When he looked up, he saw Avery's house was at the end of the block, yellow lights blazing from every window. He considered stopping until he saw Chief Templeton's black GMC round the corner. He didn't want to talk to the police again.

• • •

The smell of mu shu pork wafted through the door with Avery's father. He held up the paper bag and grinned.

"I cooked."

Avery took the bag from him and began removing the takeout boxes. "Ah, your very best recipes. Did you bring hot mustard?'

He flipped a handful of yellow packets from his coat pocket. "Bam!"

"Full-service chef."

He frowned, taking Avery's chin between his forefinger and thumb. "Looks like I should have brought a steak. Karen told me what happened. Are you okay?"

Avery shrugged and did her best mean expression. "Does it make me look tough?"

"No, it makes me nervous."

Avery stuck spoons in each of the boxes and set out two plates. "Don't be. It was Jimmy Jerold's girlfriend—I think. But since the school has a zero-tolerance policy, she'll be expelled."

"What do you mean 'you think'?"

She began heaping fried rice onto her plate. "I know she was the one who pushed me, but I'm not completely sure that this"—she pointed—"came from her." She pressed her cheek closer to her father. "Want to dust it for prints?"

"Avery, this is serious. You were in a fight."

"With a girl who's dating a murderer."

"We let him go, Avy."

She handed her father a plate. "I know." She paused. "Are you sure he didn't do it though?"

"He had a virtually airtight alibi and no motive for killing Adam or attacking Fletcher."

"Couldn't his motive be that he's an asshole?"

Chief Templeton cocked an eyebrow. "Language."

"Couldn't his motive be that he's a psychopath?"

"Sure, but given his alibi"—he stretched out the word—"he didn't do it."

A tremor of fear rushed through Avery. "So, no leads, huh?"

"We're working on a few. You really should get some more ice on that." He set his plate down and crossed the kitchen, handing Avery a bag of frozen peas.

"I'm scared, Dad. Someone killed Adam and tried to kill Fletcher. Are we safe?"

Chief Templeton took the peas and the plate from Avery's hands and pulled her into a hug. "You're always going to be safe as long as I'm here, honey. I will never let anything happen to you." He kissed the top of her head.

"I know. But—"

"The whole town is on high alert. Everyone, except you and Fletcher apparently, is taking the curfew very seriously, and I've got every officer working this case. You know Karen and Blount, Malloy and Howard—you're top priority for them."

"Yeah. Officer Blount went to see Fletcher in the hospital."

"We're doing everything we can. And we've got leads coming in by the dozen."

Avery brightened. "Anything good?"

Her father took a bite of an egg roll. "Depends what you mean by good. We've heard about aliens, forest trolls, and a bear with a mean right hook."

"Not funny, Dad."

He put both his hands on Avery's shoulders and looked her in the eye. "We're doing everything we can."

Suddenly, the smell of the Chinese food made Avery's stomach turn. She remembered the last time a police officer told her they were "doing everything" they could. It was a week after her mother died. She and her father were sitting on opposite sides of the couch, staring at a Highway Patrol officer who was assuring them that they would find the driver responsible for hitting Avery's mother, for running her off the road.

They never did.

Avery was sure she was going to be sick.

"We're bringing in a guy who says he remembers seeing Adam and Fletcher at the trailhead. We're following up on a lead about a makeshift dwelling about two miles from where the boys were—a couple of people mentioned that someone is living out there. Sounds like the same guy who freaked out a couple of college kids in town about a month ago.

"We're going to find the person that did this, Avery. I promise."

THIRTEEN

Avery and Fletcher were sitting at a corner table in the coffee shop, books spread out in front of them, the remains of a plate of french fries between them. Fletcher didn't need to study, but when Avery suggested they hang out, he agreed, not wanting to spend any more time at home. His mother had gone from fawning over him to constantly watching him.

When she wasn't, she was on the phone—with his father, Fletcher guessed—murmuring, then falling silent whenever Fletcher walked in the room. Sometimes he heard her talking to Susan, his sister, and guilt pulsed through him. The conversations with Susan never lasted long because if he was there, his mother always hung up the phone.

The press conference and the release of Jimmy Jerold did little to bolster the town's morale. The community outrage and camaraderie that Adam's murder and Fletcher's escape had inspired were waning as suspicion and fear took hold.

Two old women walked by their table, engrossed in conversation, their eyes darting around as they took in the other patrons.

"I don't know what this town is coming to," Avery heard one old lady say. "Just yesterday I heard the Morgans' car was burgled. I've lived here twenty years and nothing like that ever happened before."

"That's because crimes against cars aren't burglaries," Avery huffed under her breath.

Fletcher looked up from his biology book. "What did you say?"

"Nothing." Avery waved at the air. "It's just that it's not burglary if it has to do with a car. Burglary is breaking into a dwelling; larceny is for a car."

Fletcher smiled. "You sure know a lot."

Avery felt her cheeks warm and her stomach flutter. "Sorry. It comes from being the daughter of a cop."

"Don't apologize. It's kind of cool. What else do you know about?"

"It's illegal to plow your field with an elephant in North Carolina, and the only two things you can legally throw out of your car here are water and chicken feathers."

Fletcher nodded, impressed. "Helpful tidbits for North Carolina farmers or Californian chicken carpools."

"I also know that crime isn't really going up around here. Everyone is just talking about it more since…" Her eyes flicked to Fletcher's, then returned to her notebook. "Well, you know."

Fletcher's fingers went to his forehead. He didn't have to wear the bandage anymore, but he still found himself absently touching the scar on his forehead.

"Yeah, well, I wish people would stop talking about it." He glanced around the café. "I wish people would stop talking about everything."

Avery reached out and touched his hand, her fingers gentle. She squeezed gingerly. "My dad is going to figure out who did this and stop him."

Fletcher pulled his hand away, not meaning for it to seem as jerky as it did. "It would be a whole lot easier if I could just remember what the hell happened."

Avery tapped her fingers against the table. "It'll come back, you know."

"What will?"

"The memories."

"Yeah, maybe."

Avery held his gaze, biting her lower lip. She sighed, then edged a textbook out from the stack in front of her and flipped to a page tipped with a bright-pink Post-it note. "This is all about how the brain can shut out memories that the mind might not be ready to deal with. You know, traumatic stuff."

Fletcher glowered. "I'm not crazy."

Avery flushed again. "That's not what I'm saying. It's not about being crazy. It's about the brain wanting to protect itself. Fletch, what happened in the woods must have been horrifying."

"Yeah," Fletcher said, teeth clenched. "But I survived." Guilt infected every inch of him. He felt certain the universe would right itself. Adam was the golden child. Adam should have been the one to escape, not him. "Barely."

Fletcher looked away, not wanting to see the earnestness in Avery's clear blue eyes. She pushed the book toward him, completely undeterred.

"This says memories of trauma may come all at once or little by little, but the memories will come back."

Fletcher's mouth went dry although he had been sipping a Coke. He didn't want the memories to come back—not little by little, or all at once. As much as he wanted Adam's killer caught, he didn't want to relive any more of what had happened that day. He didn't think he could take it.

"I…"—he licked his lips nervously—"I don't know if I want them to."

Avery's gaze hardened, then softened. She swallowed. "I guess I never thought about how it would affect you. The memories coming back, I mean."

"I want to help Adam."

"I know."

Fletcher looked at his lap, his eyes moist. "But I feel safer if I don't remember what happened."

The bells over the coffeehouse door jingled and a couple walked in, letting in a burst of cold fall air.

"That's just horrendous," the woman said.

"I can't believe someone would do that. Can you imagine how the Marshalls must feel seeing that, after all they've been through?"

Both Avery and Fletcher straightened.

"Excuse me," Avery said, standing. "What about the Marshalls?"

The woman gave Avery the once-over before her lips quirked into a small smile. "Are you the police chief's daughter?"

Avery nodded. "Yeah—"

The man said, "It's the memorial for Adam. It was a makeshift memorial but still, someone destroyed it. Horrible." He clucked his tongue. "Cowardly."

"What do you mean, destroyed it?" Fletcher asked.

The woman chimed in. "Just tore it apart. Broke votives that had been left with the flowers."

"Shredded the ribbons. Even tore up the pictures of Adam. Awful."

Fletcher and Avery exchanged a look and simultaneously began to gather their things.

"We need to check this out," Avery said to him. Then, to the woman, "Does anyone know who did it? Or when it happened?"

The woman shrugged.

"No, I don't think so," she said. "But it must have been some-time late last night or early this morning."

• • •

Avery flinched against the cold air that slapped her cheeks when she and Fletcher power walked toward Adam's memorial.

"Oh God."

The corner that had once been festooned with ribbons, teddy bears, pictures, posters, sport memorabilia, and candles was a disheveled mess. The pictures and notes were torn, crumpled, and scattered over the sidewalk and street. The few bears and stuffed animals that remained were sliced and ruined, tufts of cotton stuffing poking through shredded bear bellies, ears removed, button eyes gouged out.

The candles had all been kicked over, shattered glass showered across the concrete sidewalk.

"Who would do something like this?"

Avery stepped closer, broken glass crunching under her sneakers. One of the candleholders—one with an angel on the front—was split down the middle, a feathered wing on each half. It looked as though someone had tried to piece it together again, but the angel's face remained downcast, arms outstretched to nothingness.

• • •

Fletcher's mom was at the door the moment he turned his key in the lock. Her eyes were wide and hugged by bluish bags. She always seemed to be clutching a coffee mug these days and poking her head into Fletcher's room every hour or so.

"Fletcher, honey, there you are. I was worried about you."

"Sorry, Mom. I texted you. Didn't you get it?"

Mrs. Carroll absently patted the sagging pockets on her sweater. "Are you okay?" She stepped toward him, pressing her palm against his face and studying it as though waiting for a story to unfold. He shrugged her off.

"I'm fine, Mom. Can you relax? I'm all right."

"At the news conference yesterday Chief Templeton said they let that boy go. That Jerold fellow." She pulled one of the curtains aside, peering out the window as if Jimmy would be out there waiting. "I don't think you should be out alone anymore, Fletcher. Not right now."

The anger was starting to pulse along Fletcher's veins, making his fingers twitch and his jaw clench. "I'm fine, Mom."

"You need to be okay, hon."

Fletch whirled, leveling his eyes on his mother. "I'm fine. What happened, *happened*. I can't go back, I can't change it, but I'm still the same kid, okay? I'm tired of you treating me like I'm going to fall apart at any minute."

Mrs. Carroll took two steps back, blinking. "I won't be sorry for worrying about you, Fletcher. I won't be sorry for being your mother."

Fletcher grunted and ran up the stairs, slamming his bedroom door behind him. He paced, kicking the foot of his bed as tears threatened to fall. "What the hell happened, Adam? What the fuck happened out there, man?"

Fletcher didn't remember falling asleep. His mother must have checked on him and turned out his lights because when he woke, it was pitch-dark. He was still wearing his clothes, and an afghan had been thrown over him. A glass of water and his pill on the nightstand were illuminated by the blue numbers of his alarm clock. Fletcher sat up and cleared his throat. He felt as if he had slept with his mouth wide-open.

He reached for the pill and the water but stopped when he heard the door downstairs. It had a thick brass knob that rattled any time it was turned. It was rattling now. Was someone trying to get into his house?

When he stepped into the hallway, the noise stopped. The only sound was Fletcher's own breathing.

Then someone tapped on the downstairs window.

He snatched the baseball bat he kept propped against his desk and slung it over his shoulder, stepping quickly but softly, hugging the walls. He passed his mother's bedroom door and nudged it open with his shoulder. She was cocooned in her blankets, head and shoulders covered like a shroud, taking only a snippet of space in the big bed.

Fletcher struggled to keep his own breath steady.

He picked his way down the stairs toward the scratching sound.

It's nothing, a voice inside him said. *I'm making it up.*

Then he heard the window slide open on the rail.

Someone was outside his house.

The living room seemed darker than it had ever had been, and Fletcher waited for his eyes to adjust. He didn't know how long he waited before the glass exploded, shattering all around him and raining down on him.

He felt a piece of glass slice his cheek. He felt hands on him and he swung.

He could feel the bat make contact with something hard and solid. He heard someone groan as a familiar heat blazed up Fletcher's spine.

Fight, fight, fight.

He swung again, this time missing and spinning in a circle. Glass crunched under his bare feet.

Someone jumped on him.

It's happening again.

Fletcher began to scream.

FOURTEEN

The ring of the phone cut through her sleep, and Avery launched out of bed, stumbling across her room. She threw open the bedroom door and saw her father rush by, clipping his gun belt around his waist, cell phone pressed to his ear.

"Forty-two, forty-two Sagebrush Lane," he was repeating back to the person on the phone. "On my way."

"Dad—"

He held a hand out to her. "Back to bed, Avy. I gotta go in. Keep all the doors locked."

Avery's throat tightened. "Dad, Dad, what's going on?" She followed behind him, her bare feet slapping the stairs. "What happened?"

The chief turned around and landed a kiss on the side of her forehead. "I don't know yet, hon. Just go back to bed. Everything will be fine." He shut the door behind him, the sound of the lock tumbling a stark echo.

Avery stood in the kitchen, the chill from the cold linoleum creeping up her legs. "Forty-two, forty-two Sagebrush Lane," she mumbled into the darkness. "Fletcher's house." She started to tremble.

• • •

Fletcher wished the police would turn off their lights. They splashed overhead, washing the walls with blue and red in a rhythmic pattern that made his headache worse.

He perched at the edge of the living-room sofa, the one reserved for company that never visited them, while the paramedic used extra-long tweezers to pull tiny pieces of glass from his feet. Fletcher didn't make a sound.

"Did you get a look at him, son?"

Chief Templeton spoke slowly, his head cocked like they actually were father and son and the rest of the scene—a half-dozen cops poking through the wreckage of the broken window, his mother hugging herself and shaking while she cried—wasn't actually happening. Fletcher wanted to ask the chief where Avery was, if she was alone while whoever broke into Fletcher's house had disappeared into the night.

Fletcher lost his concentration. "Who?"

The paramedic stopped, a piece of glass pinched between his tweezers, and looked at the chief. The chief looked at Fletcher's mother. She looked at Fletcher, then squeezed his arm. "The person who tried to break in, honey. Chief Templeton is asking if you saw him."

Fletcher frowned. He suddenly couldn't remember if he was dreaming or awake.

His mother squeezed his arm again. "Fletcher?"

The sounds. The broken glass. He shook his head. "No, sir. It was dark. The whole thing happened so fast."

There were no dark spots in Fletcher's memory this time. He just wasn't sure what happened when the window exploded.

"Chief?" An officer Fletcher sort of recognized—they were all starting to look the same—pointed a gloved hand at something cradled in the heavy pile carpet. "Looks like this is what came through the window."

It was a rock, oblong and gray, completely unspectacular.

The chief nodded. "Thanks, Blount." He turned back to Fletcher. "So you said someone tried the door and then was able to push the window open—but they still threw a rock."

Fletcher shrugged and his mother threw her arms around him. He stiffened as she pulled him close. She snuffled a little and Fletcher wished everyone would just leave him alone.

"I don't really know what happened."

"Isn't it obvious?" Mrs. Carroll said, suddenly full of angst. "Whoever hurt Adam is coming back for Fletcher. He was going to sneak in, but he probably saw Fletcher around the curtains in the window and got spooked. Maybe he just wanted to do some damage, wanted us to know he was here." Her eyes swept her ruined living room. "He wants us to know that he's waiting." A sob lodged in her throat and tears welled in her eyes. "I want to know what you're going to do about this, Chief Templeton. What are you doing to protect my son?"

• • •

"Are you going to tell me what happened last night?" Avery stared at her father's profile as he drove her to school.

He pointed to his eye and said, "I could ask you the same thing."

Avery glanced at her reflection in the vanity mirror, shrinking back at seeing the stripe of purple underneath her right eye. It was healing from the school incident, albeit slowly. "I told you what happened. And isn't the reporting party supposed to remain anonymous? How come this chick went after me?"

Her father shrugged. "It's a small town, Avy. Not only that, but you were one of only two people who could have reported it."

She gingerly touched the bridge of her nose. "Noted."

"But don't let that stop you from reporting all crime you encounter."

Avery flashed her dad a halfhearted salute. "Thank you for that public service announcement. Next time, remind me to ask for a bodyguard. Now, back to what I was saying—"

"Or back to what I was saying. You should always report a crime when you see one and, in particular, if you're the chief of police's daughter, you should try not to be a part of a crime."

Avery started to protest, but her father continued.

"You broke a citywide curfew that night, Avery. A curfew that was put in place for a very valid reason."

She took a deep breath and stared out the side window. "I thought that we already—"

Her father pinned her with a glare, and Avery promptly shut her mouth.

"You're lucky that Jimmy didn't do more when you ran into him."

"I know, Dad."

"Don't brush this off. This isn't like you. You know better."

Avery bit her bottom lip. "I was just trying to be a friend to Fletcher. I didn't really think beyond that. I'm sorry, Dad. I really am. It won't happen again."

"It'd better not. I understand you wanted to be there for Fletcher, and I think that's really admirable of you. But come on, Avy, be supportive in well-lit, public places during regular business hours. *Capiche?*"

There was a long silence and Avery wondered if she should push her luck. She decided to try.

"So, what happened at Fletch's last night?"

The chief cleared his throat, focusing on the road in front of them.

"Please, Dad? Fletcher's my friend. Adam was my friend." Avery didn't mean for her voice to tremble. "Please?"

Chief Templeton didn't blow out his usual sigh. "It looks like someone tried to break into the Carrolls' house last night. Fletcher may have interrupted the suspect, because the guy tossed a rock through the window and then went after Fletcher."

Avery felt her fried egg on toast sitting like a stone in her gut. "Is he okay?"

The chief nodded sharply. "He seems to be."

"But?" Avery prompted her father.

"But what?"

"You're doing that thing. You have a suspicion."

Avery's father turned to look at her, and she pointed to the road. "What thing are you talking about?"

"You grit your teeth when you're not telling me stuff."

"I don't—"

"Dad!" Avery rolled her eyes and Chief Templeton smiled.

"Very good, grasshopper."

"So what aren't you telling me? Did Fletcher get a look at the guy? Do you have a suspect?"

"No. The assailant was gone before my guys were on the scene. No fingerprints were left behind. Nothing. But there was a significant amount of damage." He shook his head. "I don't know what kind of monster we're dealing with, Avy, but I want you to steer clear."

"Of the 'monster' or of Fletcher?"

Chief Templeton didn't answer.

FIFTEEN

He should have been used to everyone looking at him by now. He had done two interviews for the newspaper and one for the local TV station—although that one was mostly cutaways of the forest and snippets of people talking about old cases. But Fletcher couldn't get used to kids paying so much attention to him.

Girls batted their eyelashes and threaded their arms through his, purring and asking him if he was okay. He couldn't get used to Adam's jock friends fist-bumping him like they were old buddies or giving him that weird little head jerk of acknowledgment in the hall. He couldn't get used to the whispers, the ones that sounded so soft but rang out so clearly—*killer...killer...killer*. When he'd turn to see who was saying it, the kids around him would look at him, though their mouths never moved.

It was even worse today.

When he came downstairs, his mother's hands were trembling. "You should probably stay home today, honey."

Fletcher shook his head. The house now had a giant piece of

plywood fitted over the broken window, which made it feel like a prison. Fletcher pushed away the slice of toast his mother set on the table in front of him.

• • •

When Fletcher saw Avery in the hall, her eyes went wide. The news of the previous night's attack hadn't spread yet, but he knew that *she* knew. She made a beeline for him.

"Hey, Fletch." She pulled him out of the flow of students. "You okay?"

"Did your dad tell you what happened?"

Avery looked around. "A little bit. Did he—" She reached out and touched his swollen cheekbone, her fingers so soft and gentle. "Are you okay?"

There was a crackling overhead and then the three chimes that signaled an announcement. Some kids stopped and cocked their heads toward the speakers, but most just continued ambling through the halls.

"Ladies and gentlemen," Principal Corben's disembodied voice started, "there will be a memorial to celebrate Adam Marshall's life this Friday at noon."

The principal blathered on about the location and logistics, but Avery stopped listening. Her eyes were fixed on Fletcher, on his vacant expression. She watched him swallow, his Adam's apple bobbing. The color slowly drained from his face, and Avery remembered what she had felt when her mother died. The community had "memorialized" or "commemorated" her mother's life, which included people dressed in their Sunday best with handkerchiefs pressed to their eyes or noses, and giant sprays of ugly flowers with ribbons with meaningless phrases like "peaceful rest" and "heartfelt sympathies."

It was as if they were honoring someone else's life—not her mother's—because Avery had never seen half the people who attended. And her mother would have rolled her eyes at the cheesy, inspirational songs that were played, and the finger sandwiches and punch—two things her mother never touched—that were served.

The three tones sounded again at the end of Principal Corben's announcement, and Avery grabbed Fletcher's arm. "Do you really want to go to class?"

Going to class had been all he wanted, but now he just wanted to feel Avery's touch. He didn't mind when *she* looked at him. He liked her attention.

"Where can we go?"

Her blue eyes scanned the rapidly emptying hall. She pulled him along the wall and out one of the side doors. "Come on!"

She took off at a dead sprint, her backpack bobbing behind her. Fletcher ran to keep up, mildly surprised that Avery Templeton—search-party team lead, daughter of the chief of police—had a little bad girl in her. He was starting to like her even more.

"Okay," she said breathing heavily and slowing to a walk. "We're officially off school property."

Fletcher glanced around. "Isn't the student parking lot considered school property?"

She cocked an eyebrow, and he recognized the expression as the same one the police chief made during interviews. But while the chief's look was pure authority, even with her hands on her hips and her legs spread slightly, Avery looked like a little girl trying to be big.

"Fine. We're officially off the learning part of school property."

"Ah, manipulating the scene. Very nice."

She rolled her eyes. "Did you drive?"

Fletcher felt his cheeks burn red. "Uh, no. My mom insists on driving me now. What about you?"

Avery jammed her hands in the pockets of her jeans and shrugged. "I don't have a car." She said something else under her breath and Fletcher leaned in to her.

"What'd you say?"

"I don't have a car."

"After that."

She looked away, tightened her ponytail, and hiked her backpack higher on her shoulders. "I don't know how to drive."

Fletcher felt himself smile. "Are you ashamed? It's not a big deal."

Avery looked stunned, her expression hardening to anger. "I'm not ashamed. What do I need to drive for anyway? There's nowhere to go in this stupid town anyway."

"I thought you were in driver's ed with Adam last year."

She shrugged him off. "Cars are death traps."

"You know what happened to your mom was an accident."

Avery's nostrils flared. "I know that."

Fletcher held up his hands, palms out. "Hey, I'm sorry." He stopped talking when Avery hitched her chin and started walking toward the edge of the lot. He jogged to catch up with her, and they fell into a companionable silence for several blocks.

"I can teach you, you know," Fletcher said finally.

Avery thought of the calm way Fletcher went about things, and her mind started to change about him—slightly.

She stopped and faced him, her expression a mix of indignation and a slight hint of curiosity. "I need coffee."

•••

Fletcher wasn't the type to go out for coffee. He *was* the type to cut school, and he did that on a pretty regular basis, but not for the double latte whatever-and-ever that Avery sat in front of him. Hers was some chocolate-looking icy concoction with a swath of whipped cream and chocolate syrup, and she dove into it, sucking on the straw until her cheeks hollowed out.

He just moved his straw around and swirled his finger through the rings of condensation on the table. He liked to think that the feeling of excitement he felt was from sitting across the table from a girl as pretty and cool as Avery Templeton, but he knew the tension in his stomach wasn't that.

"So, has your dad talked to you about Adam's case?"

Avery's eyebrows disappeared into her hair and she put her drink down. "What do you mean?"

Fletcher shrugged and took a big sip of his coffee, the cold making his head hurt. "Brain freeze," he said, trying to change the subject.

Avery smiled but kept her gaze steady. "What do you mean? He doesn't tell me all that much. He's big on confidentiality and not jinxing an open case." She took another swing of her drink. "Or maybe it's that he's too busy bugging me to finish my homework to tell me anything interesting. Why do you ask?"

"Nothing. I was just"—he paused and took another sip of the drink he really kind of hated—"making conversation."

"Have you remembered anything?"

That caught Fletcher by surprise, and he held the coffee in his mouth for an extra beat before responding. "Not really."

Avery scooted her chair over so they were shoulder to shoulder rather than face-to-face. She brushed up against him, and he cursed the heat that washed over his cheeks. "How about the blackouts? Are you still having them?"

How did she know about the blackouts? He racked his mind, trying to remember when he'd told her, *what* he'd told her.

"I haven't had them too much more lately."

"And is your memory still…blocked?"

Immediately, flashes of that day snapped through his mind: running up the trail behind Adam, slugging a bottle of water so fast it dribbled down his chin and shirt, his hand clenching a fistful of Adam's shirt.

His jaw tightened so hard that his teeth ached. Why would he remember grabbing a fistful of Adam's shirt?

"Fletcher?" Avery waved a hand in front of his face, her drink forgotten. "Fletch?"

"I-I remember grabbing Adam by the shirt." The words were out before he could filter them, before he could figure out what was going on. He could suddenly feel the ache in his forearm as he pulled Adam. It was as if he could feel the soft flannel fabric of Adam's red-and-black-checked shirt.

Avery's eyes were wide. "Really? Why were you doing that?"

Fletcher saw blood spurting. Heard screaming—his, Adam's. Terror had overtaken him, made him leave his body. Adam lying prone, a soft, primitive moan escaping his parted lips. Fletcher on the ground, unable to move, powerless to help his dying friend.

I was awake while Adam was dying.

He could have helped Adam. He could have. His stomach quivered. He stood, a bead of sweat rolling down his cheek.

"I have to go."

"Hey, Fletch—wait!"

He could hear Avery yelling behind him, the confusion and surprise evident in her voice. But Fletcher was running. His thighs ached and his calves burned, but the pain was good. He had to get away—from everyone who was watching him, from Avery, from everything.

He didn't stop running until he got home.

• • •

Avery blinked at Fletcher's empty chair and forgotten drink. *What the heck?*

Her reverie was cut short by the two college kids behind the counter and the volume on the overhead TV ratcheting up.

"They're talking about that kid who died in the woods."

The *Dan River Daily News* anchor was perched on the edge of a mustard-colored couch, her too-red lips pursed as she nodded at the woman across from her. That woman was Adam's mother. A news ticker cut across the bottom of the screen: Dan River Police Admit No Leads in Child Murder Case.

Avery listened to Mrs. Marshall.

"I just don't think the police department is doing all it can to find my son's killer. And that's putting every child in our community in danger."

A flare of anger coursed through Avery. Mrs. Marshall hadn't had to eat a silent dinner every night. She hadn't seen Chief Templeton's exhaustion, the vacant expression as he chewed, the slow way he plodded up the stairs as if his whole body were weighed down by Adam's case.

"I just think there are a lot of avenues they aren't exploring," Adam's mother went on. "What about the other child my Adam was with?"

"Fletcher Carroll?" the news anchor asked.

Mrs. Marshall pressed a handkerchief to her nose and nodded primly, a fresh wave of tears flooding her eyes.

"Is Mr. Carroll a suspect?"

Avery's stomach dropped.

She remembered Fletcher in the hospital. Saw the way he moved, protecting his broken limbs. She saw the fresh cuts and bruises.

If so, then who hurt Fletcher?

Avery grabbed her backpack and made for the door, passing the counter and hearing a snippet of conversation on her way.

"I thought that other kid was weird," the barista was saying. "He totally could have killed Adam."

SIXTEEN

Avery pushed the macaroni in wide circles on her plate as she sat at the dinner table. She had every light on in the house, and though the heat was kicked up to nearly eighty, she couldn't shake the chill that had settled in her bones. Her thoughts were on Fletcher and the way he seemed to stare off into nothingness when Adam was mentioned.

Although she tried to drown them out, the words from the barista swirled in her mind: *I thought that other kid was weird. He totally could have killed Adam.*

She had tried to speak with her father when she got home, but she kept getting his voice mail. Even Connie at the police department, who usually put Avery right through, told her that Chief Templeton was "unreachable." So Avery waited, her pulse a constant thunder.

The sound of her father's GMC pulling into the driveway snapped her back to reality, and she dumped her plate in the sink, quickly shoving her untouched dinner down the drain.

"Hey, sweetie," her father said, peeling off his rain-slicked jacket and shaking a fine mist from his hat. He kissed Avery on the forehead, then gestured toward the refrigerator. "Anything decent in there for dinner?"

"The mac and cheese isn't hairy yet."

The chief retrieved the casserole dish while Avery handed him a plate. "You eat?" he asked.

Avery nodded, taking a ginger ale from the fridge. She popped the top and took a long swig. The carbonation burned her stomach but calmed the waves of nausea.

Her father put his plate on the table. "Hey, sit with me," he said, his cheek full of macaroni.

"Anything new on Fletcher's case?" she asked carefully.

The chief chewed. "We're working on a few leads."

Avery tapped her fingers. "Is it true that you think Fletcher might be a suspect?"

"Avy, you know we consider every angle."

She glared.

"It's my job to do a thorough investigation."

"Dad," she started.

He cut her off smoothly. "Any gangs at your school?"

Avery nearly shot ginger ale through her nose. "Gangs? What are you talking about?"

Her father chewed slowly, his eyes fixed on her. "So?"

"You're serious? No, Dad, though Dan River is obviously a booming metropolis"—Avery rolled her eyes—"as far as I know, there are no gangs running rampant, running meth through the Applebee's or whatever."

He didn't smile. "I'm serious, Avy. Maybe not full-fledged gangs. What about any kids talking about gangs, gang affiliation, maybe even just off-the-cuff?" He unfolded a white piece of paper from his pocket and smoothed it on the table in front of Avery. It was a photocopy of hand-drawn symbols—two sets of dice, some stylized pitchforks, a few numbers in bubbly, funky scroll.

"Have you seen anything like this? Could be on binders, book bags, just around the school or grounds."

Avery pushed the paper back. "What is all this about?"

Chief Templeton cleared his throat. "One of the theories we're working on"—he raised his eyebrows and fixed his gaze on Avery in his *this doesn't leave this room* stare—"is that Fletcher or another suspect maybe killed Adam to gain entry into a gang or at a gang's behest."

Anger fisted her hands, almost unconsciously. "Are you kidding? First of all, 'at a gang's behest'? You don't talk like that. And you know as well as I do that Fletcher isn't involved with gangs. There are no gangs in this stupid town, and Fletcher *didn't* do this, Dad. He didn't!"

"Avy—"

"No!" She was breathing hard now, tears burning behind her eyes. "The real killer is out there, probably trying to figure out which one of us is going to be next, and you guys can't see it because you have your noses so far—"

"Avery Elise Templeton, you better think long and hard about how—or if—you want to finish that sentence," her father said. "You should consider that up in your room."

Avery stomped upstairs and slammed her door, hot tears stinging her cheeks. She and her dad had argued before and she had always gotten over his unyielding responses, but this was different. This wasn't a halter top or a later curfew. This was her friend and it was his life. She fired up her computer and started searching anything she could think of: serial killers, spree killers, people who kill in the woods. And then, when the night had gone from dark to an impenetrable, inky black, she searched something else—*trauma, memories, blacking out.*

SEVENTEEN

Avery's father knocked and pushed the door open while he slid into his DRFPD Windbreaker. "I got a call; I've got to go in."

"Is it about Adam?"

"No." He shook his head. "I don't know when I'll be back, but the house will be locked up behind me. Stay inside. No funny business. You're still on my list." There may have been an edge to Chief Templeton's voice, but it didn't extend to his eyes. He turned and Avery listened as he clopped down the stairs in his boots and pulled the garage door shut behind him.

The entire house fell into an eerie silence.

Avery crossed her bedroom and peered out the window to watch her father's car pull away.

The streetlight cast a weak shadow on the clutch of trees across the street from their house. Something moved in the shadows. She clicked off the overhead light to get a better look, squinting.

"I'm being stupid," she mumbled.

There was a clap of thunder, and Avery's heart started clanging like a fire bell. She clutched her chest and let it pound, then started to laugh as the sky broke and sheets of rain fell.

"Oh my gosh, I'm the biggest wimp!" she said, laughing to herself. She went back to her computer and clicked a link for something called "dissociative amnesia."

Patients with dissociative amnesia experience disruptions in their memories. They have recurrent episodes in which they forget important information or events, usually connected with severe trauma or stress.

"Okay," she said, biting her lower lip. "That sounds like what Fletch has." She centered her mouse over another link. "Now, what can we do about it?"

Dissociative amnesia patients experience a high susceptibility to hypnosis, which can unlock painful or unwelcome memories.

Avery scrawled the word "hypnosis" with a big question mark on her scratch pad. For a town that had just gotten a Starbucks, having a hypnotist within city limits was more than unlikely. She went back to her Google search, and the links that populated her list gave her a chill.

Mental disorders…blackouts…schizophrenia…

The sky cracked again, and this time Avery went to shut her window. A fork of lightning cast a white glow over the trees, which swayed in the wind. Avery blinked. She swore she saw movement. "There is nothing there, Avery. Stop being a baby."

But she couldn't shake the feeling that someone was out there, watching her. She tried to go back to her computer, but her fingers were trembling. She might be the chief of police's daughter, but even she got the heebie-jeebies. And when she did, they were hard to shake. She grabbed her cell phone.

Fletcher answered on the first ring.

• • •

Fletcher didn't know where his mom had gone. She'd said something about a meeting or a session, but he hadn't been paying attention. Her voice had mixed with the cacophony spitting from the television set. Whenever he was home, the TV was on. He didn't have a favorite show or even one he liked very much, but the noise soothed him. Or maybe it just drowned out the buzzing in his mind.

The phone cut through the din, and he smiled when he saw Avery's number on the screen.

"Hey, Avery."

"Hey, Fletch." She was silent for an uncomfortable beat while Fletcher considered what to say. What could he talk about that wasn't stupid? "So I was thinking about your blackouts again," she said.

He deflated, having hoped somehow that she was calling just to say hey, that he could be a normal guy having a conversation with a girl about music or movies or what to do Saturday night. "Yeah?"

"You know the book I showed you? Well, I was also reading online that your brain can trap memories and stuff."

He let out a slow sigh. "Repressed memories?"

"Yeah." Avery sounded way too chipper on the other end of the phone. Fletch tried to imagine her sitting at home, her bedspread and walls painted something cheerful and girly like yellow or hot pink. "I read that hypnosis can possibly unlock those memories."

Her voice didn't sound as cheery now, and Fletcher's thoughts about Avery in her bedroom turned dark. "And?"

"I thought maybe you might want to do that. You know, to help Adam."

Without knowing why, Fletcher felt himself bristle. Adam. It was always about Adam.

Adam was your friend.

A sharp pain stabbed behind his eye, and he sucked in a breath. "Are you okay?"

Fletcher pressed his fingertips against his eyeball. "Yeah. I get headaches now because of the hit to the head."

Avery was silent for a minute and Fletcher almost thought she had hung up.

"I'm really sorry," she said finally.

He shrugged, though she couldn't see it, and looked around his darkened house. The glow from the TV was minimal; whatever show he was watching featured incredibly good-looking people looking pained. There was silence on the phone but he could hear Avery breathing—short, shallow breaths that let him know something was brewing. She was considering something heavy in her head. Fletcher let himself think that maybe she liked him, that maybe she'd called to tell him. His mind raced and he thought he should ask her out, make some sort of plan.

She cleared her throat and thoughts pinged in his brain. A movie? A walk? Just hang out? Then she spoke.

"Don't you want to know what happened that day?"

• • •

Avery waited for Fletcher to answer, but his phone began plinging with the cacophony of dying battery sounds and cut out at the same instant that Avery was plunged into darkness. She scuttled to the window. The houses that Avery could see were dark too, windows blank and gaping like open mouths.

Her phone blared through the blackness, the glowing face slightly ominous in the dark.

"Hey, Dad."

"You okay, Avy?"

A lump started to grow in Avery's throat and she wanted to beg him to come home or to hide under the covers until the lights turned back on—or at least until the thunder stopped its ruthless shuddering—but she was sixteen and she wasn't afraid of the dark. At least she shouldn't be. She sniffed and went to her desk drawer, pulling out a heavy Maglite flashlight and clicking it on.

"A-okay."

"You know there's—"

"An emergency flashlight in my desk drawer and two in the linen closet right next to the box of emergency candles, extra batteries, and that hand radio thing."

"It's a ham radio."

"Whatever, Dad. I'm good though."

Avery could hear the smile in her father's voice. "That's my girl. Look, the storm has gotten pretty bad. There are a lot of power outages. We're going to check for flooding. You need to stay put."

Instinctively, Avery glanced toward the clock on her nightstand.

"Um, it's midnight. I guess I'll have to cancel the middle-of-the-night shopping trip I have planned, but okay."

"Avery…" A fake warning voice.

"I'm fine, Dad. Go save the world. Be safe."

"And you go to bed."

"Bye, Dad."

The eeriness of the situation was gone. It was just a blackout from a stormy night in Dan River. "No big deal," Avery said to herself as she pulled her laptop into bed with her.

And then something thunked.

It came from downstairs and was half muffled by carpet, but it was definitely a thump. Avery sat upright, her palms beginning to sweat despite the chill that cut through her.

"It's nothing," she told herself.

She edged herself back into her bed, pressing her head into her pillow. Avery clenched her eyes shut. There was another crash. This one sounded like the splintering of a piece of furniture getting knocked over.

Avery kicked off her covers, her heart threatening to thunder right out of her chest.

"Dad?" Avery called, her voice sounding tinny and small. "Dad, are you home?"

The noise of someone breaking things came from downstairs. A sob lodged in her throat.

Steeling herself, she gripped the Maglite and breathed deeply, certain her dad—if he were here—would kill her for what she was about to do, but she couldn't ball herself up in her bedroom and wait for whoever was downstairs to find her. She hugged the wall like she had seen in every cop movie. She held the Maglite like a baseball bat and kept it off, concealing her presence with the darkness.

Each time her bare foot made contact with a stair, she forced herself to breathe, a long, whooshing in and out like she had learned in yoga class. It was supposed to nourish and steady the mind, but it was making her light-headed. When she was on the last step, a gust of wind tore through the house. Avery shuddered. Whoever was in the house must have left the door open, probably for a quick escape.

With thoughtless rage tearing through her, Avery clicked on the Maglite and shone the bright beam into the living room screaming, "My dad is the chief of police. You better start running, asshole!"

Avery sucked in a shaky breath. "Oh my God."

The lamp from the end table was on the floor, its bulb shattered. The half-dozen family pictures were on the ground too. Another gust of wind snapped the pages of the magazines she and her dad had on the coffee table—a catalog for police gear, an out-of-date *CosmoGirl*, a circular from the grocery store. But the destruction wasn't what was terrifying to Avery.

It was the windows.

Every single one, the whole bank lining the wall, was wide open, with curtains billowing like ghosts in the wind and wet leaves sticking to the screens like hands trying to claw their way into the house.

EIGHTEEN

"You sound just like my dad," Avery snapped.

Fletcher had been awake and out the door early, the world heavy with that weird sense of eerie renewal that always happened after a storm. Avery was mad at him, stomping ahead.

"I'm only saying it was possible," he said, trying to make his voice light.

Avery rolled her eyes as they entered the school together. "I guess it *could* have been a dream," she said finally. "But it felt so real. I know I walked down the stairs. I *know* I saw all those windows open. I felt the wind on my face."

"But didn't you call your dad? And then you said you went downstairs…"

Avery rolled her eyes and picked at the seam on her jeans. "Yeah. I went downstairs and waited for him."

"And?"

"Everything was fine down there. As if it never happened."

"Maybe because it never did."

Avery's eyes flashed and Fletcher flinched. "But it was real. I can't believe you don't believe me. We know that someone is out there, someone who attacked you and killed Adam. Maybe that person is lurking around town."

Fletcher didn't want to think that whoever had come after him and Adam would go after Avery. If Avery got hurt, it would be all his fault. Just like what happened to Adam...

"So did your dad check around or something?"

"He didn't find anything. Outside or inside. He thinks..."— Avery looked away, then glanced back at Fletcher—"that I am probably just freaked out, that I had a bad dream."

Her cheeks flushed pink. Fletcher liked it.

"But the lamp was missing," she hurried on. "The one that was broken on the floor? It was missing when I got up this morning."

"Did you tell your dad that?"

"Yeah. Only..."

"Only?"

Avery looked slightly annoyed but fidgeted with the strap of her backpack like she might be nervous. "I told my dad about the lamp, and he said it hadn't been there in weeks. He said he broke it awhile ago and got rid of it."

Fletcher wanted to say something to comfort her, something to let her know that he knew that batty, paranoid feeling she was describing.

"You know how it is when there is a detail you know that you're missing, but you just can't get to it?"

Fletcher stiffened and Avery apologized. "I mean...sorry. Of course you do. You—I just—"

Fletcher shook his head and shook off the comment.

"It's just weird…" she said, her words trailing off. "It was just really weird."

Fletcher grimaced. He had spent the night before trying to fall asleep, but he kept thinking about Avery, about how she'd mentioned hypnosis just before the phone died. What if he could remember what happened after he and Adam were attacked?

What if I don't want to?

The voice in his head came out of nowhere, but it shot ice water through his veins.

Adam was my friend, he repeated to himself, his teeth gritted so hard that his jaw ached.

"What's with you?" Avery asked.

Fletcher snapped back to the here and now. "It's nothing. I was just… Yeah, I know what you mean about forgetting—"

He stopped in the hallway, his words dying in his mouth. "Oh, oh my God."

Avery saw it too.

As had the large group of teens who had congregated off to the side, whispering and staring at Fletcher's locker. "KILLER" was scrawled across the metal in thick, red ink.

Fletcher felt the piece of toast he had eaten for breakfast pushing its way up his throat. He knew Avery was talking to him. He knew he should respond, but he could only stare at the word: KILLER.

Fletcher turned, only aware that Avery had her hand on his arm when he shook it off to ran for the bathroom. He went for the nearest stall, bent over, and dry heaved, tears clouding his vision, snot running from his nose.

He was a killer.

He hadn't been able to save Adam in the woods. And so the kids at school had branded him a killer. A murderer.

He heaved again, then flushed the toilet, leaning against the wall of the bathroom stall.

Why couldn't he just remember?

Lately, the visions were all the same. Adam calling out to him, then a flash of sunlight so bright it burned, then that sickening, overwhelming smell of blood. He heard Adam screaming for him: "Fletcher! Fletcher!" His shoulders screamed, his forearms burning as he swung blindly, going for some*thing* or some*one* who, in his memory, was nothing but a hazy blur. That blur killed Adam and tried to kill Fletcher too.

• • •

Avery stood in the hallway, stunned, as Fletcher strode away from the gathering crowd. "That dude is crazy," someone murmured.

"How can they even let him back in school?" someone else asked.

Avery fisted her hands, holding them so tightly that she could feel her fingernails cutting into her palms.

"Who did this?" She didn't recognize her own voice when it came out.

No one answered, but the chatter continued, students flooding over to see what the commotion was about.

Fletcher is not a murderer.

"Fletcher is not a murderer!" She screamed and a few kids nearby shot her weird looks. Tim stood in front of Avery, hands gripping the straps on his backpack.

"Avery, you should stay away from that kid." His chin jutted after Fletcher.

"He's not—" she started, but Tim's hand on her arm stopped her.

"Adam's dead." His eyes were serious. "You don't know what happened out there in the woods."

"That's just it," Avery said, jerking away from Tim's grip. "No one knows what happened out there."

Tim said, "Fletcher knows."

He disappeared into the crowd and Avery stood there, feeling very alone. These people didn't know the facts. The evidence. They didn't see Fletcher that day in the woods, his face bloodied and battered, the look of sheer and utter relief that had washed through his tired eyes when he recognized her, when he knew he was going to be saved.

They didn't find me, Avery. You did.

The late bell shot her back to reality and Avery looked around, realizing the hall was mostly empty. She ran to class, huffing by the time she reached the door.

"It's not like he couldn't have done it," a blond girl named Stacey or Sarah or something with an *S* said. "He wasn't *that* much smaller than Adam."

"Why would he?" another girl asked. "What would be the point?"

"Jealousy?" Tim was in the circle, his desk turned inward so he was facing the *S*-girl.

Avery looked around for their teacher. *They shouldn't be having this conversation*, she thought. *This isn't right.*

"Where's Ms. Holly?" she finally managed.

Kaylee spoke up from the circle. "Admin office." She held up a few newspapers and magazines. "We're supposed to talk about trial by media."

Then Avery noticed that all the desks were sectioned off into little circles, some students talking about the assignment, most typing on contraband cell phones. Her eyes went back to Kaylee, to the newspapers. One headline blared out at her: Is Fletcher Carroll a Suspect in the Marshall Murder?

Her stomach dropped into her shoes. "Why—why would you—they—think Fletcher did this? He's just a kid. A nice kid. Like us."

"It's not that we're accusing him," Tim said carefully. "We're just not excluding him as a suspect. You have to admit—"

"And just a kid?" Kaylee's eyes were hard and sharp. "Have you *seen* the news? It's full of fifteen- and sixteen-year-old murderers."

"I blame video games!" someone screamed from the back of the class.

"No, it's that rock music!" someone else yelled to a chorus of laughter.

"The devil made me do it!"

More quips. More laughter. More anger raced through Avery's veins.

"One in three kids is a sociopath, you know," Kaylee said, her gaze still fixed on Avery. She pointed to the student next to her as she counted off. "One, two…" Her last finger landed on Avery. Kaylee smiled. "Three."

Tim said, "Fletcher is seriously a sociopath."

"Psychopath."

Avery stood there, blinking and incredulous. It had been twelve days since Adam had been found dead and Fletcher wounded. Adam and Fletcher were their classmates. And now these kids were tossing around the suspicion that Fletcher was some kind of killer.

"He didn't do this," she spat out.

Kaylee turned back to Avery, her baby-blue eyes full of false innocence. "If not him, who?"

• • •

Fletcher waited in the library stacks until the bell rang. Apparently, the need for atlases and world maps wasn't huge, and he had the space to himself. No one questioned him. No one called him a killer. But the flashes were coming again. Hard. Fast.

Adam lying in the dirt, his hand outstretched. "Come on, man," Adam was saying. "Come on, man. You have to help me."

Fletcher slunk down and pulled his knees up to his chest, resting his forehead against them.

Come on, think! he commanded himself. His thoughts went to Avery and hypnosis. *Don't you want to know what happened out there?*

Panting, his breath tore through his lungs.

"Come on, Fletch!" Adam had him by the shirtfront. Tears streamed down Adam's face. "Fletcher!" He could feel the bursts of Adam's breath

washing over his cheeks, and Fletcher wondered why he couldn't see Adam clearly. It was if there was a fog between them.

His head was throbbing. His brain wasn't functioning He wasn't himself. All he could feel was the rage overtaking him.

In the library, Fletcher felt the muscles across his back tense. The sweat on the back of his neck chilled, and he shivered so hard that his teeth chattered. He wanted to sink into the library floor and disappear. Everything would be better if he just disappeared.

He thought of his mother's anguished face when he'd opened his eyes at the hospital. He thought of Avery, Chief Templeton, and Adam. He had to remember something. They were all counting on him.

He pushed himself up from the floor as the bell rang. In the hallway, he blended into the swarm of students, although he felt as if everyone were watching him, blaming him.

"Hey, Fletch," Avery said. "I've been looking all over for you."

After what had happened that morning, Avery didn't seem scared of him. Relief rushed over him. "Yeah," he said over the sound of students' voices. "I just needed some time."

She nodded.

He stared down at the toes of his sneakers—new ones, since the police had taken his old ones for "investigative purposes."

"About my locker…"

Avery cocked her head and pointed to her ears, wagging her head. "Outside," she mouthed, pushing him.

"Sorry, I couldn't hear you," he said once they were out the door.

"Look, Fletch, I've been thinking about it, and we need to figure this out. I know you don't remember much from the escape, but do you remember anything? Like other cars in the parking lot when you arrived? Anyone you saw on the trail?"

The thudding started again in his head. *Why wouldn't she just leave it alone?*

"I don't know, Avery. Your dad and the cops, they asked me a million times and I can't—"

Car tires grinding over gravel. Fletcher getting out of the car. Adam coming around and snatching up a McDonald's bag from the ground, crushing it with his fists. "People are such freaking slobs."

He did a jump shot, the wadded-up bag landing smoothly in the trash can near the trail's entrance.

"Probably that guy's lunch." Fletcher shook his head at the other car in the parking lot, a red something or other. Racing stripe down the side. Busted fender.

"There was another car in the lot, but I never saw who drove it."

Avery's eyes were saucers. "You remember that?"

Fletcher blinked. "Yeah, yeah I guess I do."

"Fletch, this is a clue. A huge clue! We have to tell my dad. Oh my God, this could blow the case wide open." Avery was very animated, like one of those kids overacting in the school play. She stopped. "Fletch, do you not realize what a major breakthrough this is?"

He swallowed, not feeling an ounce of Avery's excitement. "It was just a car."

"But it means someone else was out there on the trail with you guys and—"

"Avery—"

"Come on, Fletch. Come on. Do you remember anything else? Did you notice if it had California plates? Anything decorative around the license plate?"

Fletcher closed his eyes just to get Avery off his back. The moment he did…

"Fletch, Fletch, what the hell, man?"

The sound of flesh on flesh. Bones cracking.

An arc of blood.

"I can't see! I can't—where are you?"

Whose voice? Whose voice was that?

Blood on his hands, blood gushing from his lip.

"Fletch!"

Adam. Where was Adam?

Swing. Hit. Connect.

Swing, hit, connect.

"Fletch…" a croaked whisper.

"What if I did it?"

NINETEEN

Avery stepped back as if Fletcher's admission had physically shoved her. "Fletch, what are you talking about?"

"I can't remember. I'm trying, but…" He stared at his hands, clenching his fists, feeling the skin pull against the crisscross of scabs and stitches that remained. "What if I did it?"

Avery shook her head, a tremor going through her. "That's stupid, Fletch. That's just dumb. Adam was your friend. You wouldn't do that. You wouldn't! I know you."

Fletcher wanted to agree, but he could feel the dark inside him. It sickened him. It scared him.

"Why would you do it? There's no reason." Avery crossed her arms in front of her chest. "Don't be dumb."

"I remember Adam saying, 'Stop, stop.'" He shook his hands, which suddenly felt as if they were covered in the dirt and debris from the forest. "What if his blood was on me?"

Avery stood up straighter and gripped Fletcher by his forearms. "Listen to me, Fletch. You didn't do this. Your memories are all jumbled up, and yeah, you had blood all over you. But you also had cuts all over you. The blood was yours."

"No, Avery."

"You're a good guy. You probably were trying to help Adam. Or it could be survivor's guilt. You read about that all the time."

A knot formed in Fletcher's chest. He didn't want Avery to defend him. He didn't want her to *want* to defend him. Somehow he felt like he didn't deserve it.

Students streamed out of the building around them. Most walked straight past, but a few slowed and eyed Fletcher and Avery.

Kaylee and Stacey came out with Tim. Kaylee coughed the word "socio" into her hands. Stacey exploded into giggles. Tim laughed too but tried to turn his face away.

"Don't make him mad," one of the girls said. "We don't know what he's capable of."

Fletcher gritted his teeth.

"Fletch." Avery grabbed him by the arm again but he shook her off.

"Just stay away from me, okay?"

• • •

Avery yanked out her phone and dialed her father.

"What's up, kiddo?"

"Dad, why is everyone accusing Fletch of murder?"

"Avery—"

"It's all over school. Someone graffitied his locker, and people are calling him a sociopath. He's not a real suspect, is he?"

There was a long, uncomfortable pause, and Avery knew exactly what her father wasn't saying.

"I can't believe you."

"Avery, look. We have to examine—"

"I know, I know, all the angles," she spat.

"For now, it's probably a good idea for you to give Fletcher some space."

Avery's mouth dropped open. "Stay away from him? He's my friend! He needs me!"

"Just for a—"

"Whatever, Dad."

She hung up, knowing she was in for several choice evenings staring at her bedroom ceiling without her phone or computer, but she was miffed. How could her father believe that Fletcher could *kill* Adam? Or put her in danger?

Livid, her fingers flew over the lock combo on her bike. She shoved the lock in her backpack and started pedaling.

The sun was beginning to dip behind the trees, and the few weak, remaining beams of sunlight shaded and mottled a deep gray. It made the chill in the damp air heavy, and Avery shivered even as sweat beaded at her hairline. She pumped her legs harder.

This was one of the winding stretches of the Redwood Highway that lacked a bike lane. In the summer, it made for an agonizing, thigh-burning series of switchbacks. In the fall it was a beautiful, canopied ride, the lush trees keeping the road cool. With the roads slick and the weak streaks of light, all Avery wanted to do was get home and into a hot shower.

That was what she was thinking about when she heard the purr of the engine behind her, approaching from one of the switchbacks. She flicked on the bike's front and back lights, her two wheels blinking like a beacon, the reflectors her father insisted she attach to her backpack bouncing back headlights as the car crawled up behind her.

Avery edged herself as far to the right as she dared, casting a glance at the narrow shoulder and the slope of mountainside beyond. She hated this part of the ride and gripped one handlebar tightly, while using her other hand to wave the car around her.

It stayed a good thirty feet behind. The vibration from the motor wobbled her tires all the way through her feet. She pumped a little harder, trying to put some distance between herself and the car.

It caught up.

"Go around," she said, waving. She craned her neck to see around the bank of the next switchback, then turned toward the car, yelling, "Clear!" The gray sky was settling in, the last of the sunlight bouncing off the windshield, obscuring the driver. "Clear!" she said again.

The driver maintained his speed behind her and Avery sighed, rolling her eyes. "If you want to go ten miles an hour behind me, suit yourself, dude."

She continued pedaling, wishing she could pop in her earbuds and listen to anything other than the hum of the engine and the voices in her head. She was trying to focus on the list of phyla she was supposed to memorize for bio when the driver gunned the engine. Avery glanced over her shoulder just in time to see the car's grill kissing her back tire.

"Hey!" she yelled, wobbling on the bike. "What the hell?"

The car sunk back, but her heart slammed against her rib cage. "Jerk!"

The thunk of a heavy bass blasted from the car. The music grew closer.

Avery edged toward the outside white line, a little closer to the edge of the road, keeping her focus directly in front of her rather than on the drop a few inches from her fat, hybrid tires. A bead of sweat trickled down her back as she lifted herself from the seat to pedal faster.

"Go around, jerk!"

The car didn't pull back.

Avery cut hard to the left, whizzing over the double yellow line.

The oncoming headlights of another car nearly blinded her as it swung around the turn.

"Oh my God!"

Avery resisted the urge to let go of the handlebars and cover her face with her hands. Instead, she swerved. Her heart was ready to explode in her throat. She had no choice but to cut in front of the car that had been trailing her while the other one sped by. She prayed the driver of the car trailing was just some jerk trying to mess with her. She prayed that the long honk and the flood of headlights scared him too, and that he would hang back.

He didn't.

The car tagged her bike's back tire. Avery wobbled for what

felt like an eternity, her whole body tense as she tried to keep her bike upright. If she fell or stopped, the psycho driver would surely run her over. She had to put distance between them. She sped up. So did the driver. The next sound was the crack of her wheel against the car's fender as it folded in two and snapped free of the bike frame.

Pain exploded in her chin and palms as she scudded along the roadway. Her breath was gone. She was still sliding, still moving from the force of the hit when she saw the edge of the roadway coming up on her fast. She tried to kick out her legs, to grip the concrete to stop herself, but the remains of her bike hit her hard on the back of her head. She was airborne. She slid and rolled, then stopped a few yards down the incline.

Above her, there was a weighted silence that pricked at the back of her neck. A car door slammed, followed by the slow, loud sound of boots.

Avery tried to move her head but everything hurt. She had just enough energy to cut her eyes toward the roadway, toward the figure who rounded the car and stared down at her.

A tremor went through Avery. Would the figure approach her? There was no way she could defend herself.

Slowly the driver turned on his—or her—heel and got back in the car. Avery heard the car door slam, the rev of the engine, and the blaring radio fade as the car disappeared around the bend.

TWENTY

"Fletch, honey, you're home."

Fletcher's mother sat at the kitchen table, her hands wrapped around a coffee mug. She took off her reading glasses and neatly folded them on top of a sudoku puzzle. "How was school? Let me fix you something to eat."

Fletcher wanted the scene to be normal: a mom having an exchange with her son about school, pushing her chair back to pull some crackers out of the pantry. But there was something different about it. Maybe it was the way his mother's hands shook when she pulled out the cracker box or how she kept looking over her shoulder while she dug through the refrigerator for a block of cheese—as if she was scared to turn her back to him.

He glanced over his shoulder toward the living room where the plank of plywood was still bolted to the broken window and shifted his weight. "Did the police say anything about the other night?" The hair along his arms pricked up as he asked the question.

His mother shook her head. "No, nothing."

A palpable silence hung in the air, and Fletcher knew he should sit down or click on the TV or flip through one of the comic books stashed in his backpack. If he was occupied, maybe his mom would relax.

"Have you heard from Dad?"

His mother looked nervous and knocked over the box of crackers on the counter with her jitters. "He's fine," she said quickly. "And Susan's fine. She likes her school."

Mrs. Carroll arranged the crackers and cheese slices on a plate. She pulled a paring knife from the drawer and palmed a red apple. The sound of the knife slicing through the apple seemed deafening. Fletcher stared as the knife worked through the fruit's glossy red skin.

KILLER. He saw the word on his locker again.

Am I a killer?

His mother pulled the knife through the apple again, exposing its white flesh.

Fletcher felt his temples pulsing.

His blood rushing through his veins.

"Fletch, Fletch, man, what the hell?"

"Mom—"

She turned. "What is it, honey?"

Heart racing. Flesh meeting flesh. Pain searing in his gut. The smell of pine trees, dirt, blood.

"I think we should call Dr. Palmer."

• • •

Avery sat in her father's GMC, her bent and broken bicycle in the back. She had taken out her ponytail, picked out pieces of twigs and debris, and slicked her hair back three separate times before Chief Templeton cast her an exasperated glance.

"Are you going to tell me what happened?"

"I fell." Avery shrugged, uncertain why she felt the need to lie to her dad. She knew in her gut that the car's driver had meant to harm her. It wasn't just some guy driving around. He was after *her*—but why? Because she'd been talking to Fletcher? If she told her father, he'd overreact and never let her talk to Fletcher again. Avery was surprised at how much she didn't want that.

She had cried after the car drove off and the fear eased out of her. She had pushed herself up from the bush that had broken her fall and examined herself. Her palms were cut from skidding down the bank, but she wasn't seriously injured. Her lip felt swollen, and her left knee was skinned and visible through the new hole in her jeans.

"It was awful at school today, Dad. Everyone thinks that Fletcher killed Adam." She watched her father's profile for a reaction.

"How do you feel about that?"

Avery gawked. "How do I feel about that? You sound—you sound like—" A sob lodged in Avery's throat and the road in front of them went blurry with her tears.

He sounded like he used to after Avery's mother died, always asking psychologist-constructed questions that required more than yes or no answers, designed to "get kids talking about their feelings." She knew her father had pulled these questions word-for-word from a pamphlet that he picked up at the grief center where he forced her to see a counselor.

"I feel like that's shit, and I feel like you know it."

"Avery!"

"You have to give me some information, Dad. This is my friend—don't just tell me to stay away from him. Don't do that to me!" She was crying—great, racking sobs that made her shoulders shake and her lungs spasm.

"Avery." Her father spoke in a slow, controlled manner that only made Avery feel that much more alone.

"Someone ran me off the road today, Dad! I didn't just fall off my bike. Someone was trying to kill me, and it wasn't Fletcher! It was probably the guy who killed Adam. What if he knows I'm helping Fletch?" She heaved, hiccuped. "Why won't you tell me what's happening?"

The chief pulled the car over to the side of the road. "Avery, what are you talking about?"

The more Avery tried to calm down, the more she hiccuped-cried. "I was riding my bike and a car came up behind me, and—and—" Her body replayed the whole scenario, the way she gripped her handlebars, the way her heart raced.

"What kind of car was it?"

Avery shook her head, feeling dumb. "I don't even remember. I was too scared to get a good look. A truck maybe? No, no, like a regular car."

"A sedan?"

A car zipped past them and Avery started. That was the car! Then another car came speeding the other direction, and she was sure *that* was the one. "I don't know," she said, defeated.

Chief Templeton clicked off his seat belt and turned sideways to face his daughter. "Are you okay? Do we need to take you to the hospital?" His cheeks had an unnatural flush in them, and his eyes were concerned, like a father who thought of her before suspects and criminals.

"It was the same person who hurt Adam and Fletcher. It had to have been. Fletch said he remembered a car in the park's parking lot that day. Did he tell you that?"

• • •

Fletcher didn't remember falling asleep. He was still fully dressed and the lights in his bedroom were on, his classroom-issued copy of *A Separate Peace* looking rather dog-eared and pitiful as he rolled off it.

He yawned, wondering what woke him, when he heard his mother's voice. "Fletcher?" She sounded somewhat distant, as if she was on the landing.

"Yeah?"

"Come down here, please."

He rolled his eyes but got up anyway, trudging into the semi-dark hallway. He straightened when he saw that his mother wasn't alone on the landing. "Ma?"

His mother had changed out of her bathrobe—something she rarely did lately—and was wearing lipstick. Her hair was brushed and pinched at the nape of her neck. Two uniformed officers stood next to her.

"Hello," Fletcher said, more question than greeting.

"Fletcher, honey." His mother glided up the stairs to him and laced her arm through his, so he'd walk with her. "These are Officers Hobbs and Dawes from the police department."

"Am I in some kind of trouble?"

One of the officers shook his head. "No, son," Officer Dawes said. "This is just routine."

Fletcher slid his arm from his mother's and took a tentative step back up the stairs. "What is routine?"

Hobbs, the other cop, stepped forward and handed Fletcher's mother a piece of paper folded in thirds. She opened it and Fletcher could see the words "Search Warrant" written in fancy diploma-type scroll at the top.

"What is this?"

"It's a search warrant."

Fletcher fought down the urge to curse at the smug officer. "I know, but why?"

"It's just routine, honey." His mother parroted Officer Dawes.

"Yeah, but I already handed over my clothes and shoes and my backpack and everything I had with me that day. What else do you guys need?"

"We just need to cover all our bases, son."

Anger pinballed through Fletcher at Dawes's use of the term "son," but he kept his expression bland.

"We're going to need to search your room, the garage, and your vehicle."

"I wasn't even driving my car—" Hobbs passed Fletcher as he made his way to the bedroom. "Mom, are you going to let this happen?"

"Do you have something to hide, Mr. Carroll?"

"Fletch," he corrected. "And no. I was a victim here." He yanked up his shirtsleeve, thrusting his arm at the cop. His scar was healing pink and silvery, a zigzag across his flesh.

"It's routine so that we can be sure we have all of the details we need for our investigation." Officer Dawes held Fletcher's eye, which immediately made him feel guilty for no real reason.

He threw an angry glance at his mother, who now seemed like the cops' accomplice. "Sure. Whatever."

Officer Dawes nodded and turned toward the garage. Mrs. Carroll flashed Fletcher a smile that was meant to be apologetic or reassuring but failed on both counts. "How about I fix you some tea?"

He followed his mother to the kitchen and slumped at the dining table while she filled the teapot.

"This is lame."

"It's just—"

"Don't tell me it's routine, Ma. I have ears. I just mean, why are they wasting their time here when they should be out looking for Adam's killer?"

His mother was silent, as though setting a teapot on a burner took all her concentration. Fletcher couldn't look at her.

"Do you think they think I did this?"

She shot a look over her shoulder, her smile tight. "No, honey, of course not. They probably just need to rule you out as a suspect. Like on television."

Fletcher wanted to feel comforted, but the way his mother flittered around lately—nervously and always watching him—gave him pause. "Do *you* think I had something to do with Adam's death?"

It could have been his imagination, but Fletcher thought she paused before she answered, "Of course not, Fletcher!"

TWENTY-ONE

Avery knocked on Fletcher's door. She bounced on the balls of her feet while she waited for someone to answer. She was about to leave, figuring no one was home, when she heard movement inside.

"Avery?"

"Hey, sorry. I called your house and your cell, but no one answered." She shoved a handful of papers toward him. "You weren't in school today, so I picked up your homework."

Fletcher's expression was blank.

"I know. Exactly what you wanted, huh?"

Fletcher's face broke into a wide grin. "You're right. I would have rather had…well, just about anything else. But the delivery girl is cool so it's all right." He immediately looked down at his feet, and Avery could see his cheeks reddening—much like hers surely were.

"Can I come in?"

Fletch nodded, and she stepped into the foyer's twilight-like darkness. It was so quiet and still that it was as if no one actually lived there.

"Is it just you and your mom?" she asked. She had a vague

memory of seeing Fletcher's dad around the time they moved in. He was a slight man who shared Fletcher's square jaw and dark curls. She thought she remembered an older girl too, but it was a long time ago and Avery was reminded of how little she really knew about Fletcher.

"Yeah. You want a drink or something?"

"Sure." Avery followed Fletcher toward the kitchen, trying to pinpoint what irked her so much about the house.

Fletcher opened the refrigerator.

"You've got nothing in there!" The appliance light was glaring, making the shelves look very sparse.

Fletcher just shrugged.

Avery looked around the kitchen: no coffee cups in the sink, no cereal boxes on the counter, no ugly magnets from different states stuck to the fridge. The house was beyond pristine—it was nearly empty.

"Are you guys moving or something?"

Fletcher handed Avery a bottle of water and took one for himself. "No. My mom just doesn't like to keep a lot of stuff, I guess."

"I wish that were the case at our place. My dad is a pack rat. It's really organized but still." She grinned. "I think he wants to make sure we're prepared for the zombie apocalypse."

Fletcher smiled. "So…"

Avery unscrewed the cap on her bottle and took a long sip. "So…"

"Why are you here?"

She felt as if she had just sucked down lighter fluid.

Fletcher's expression immediately changed to one of apology, and he held out his hands. "I didn't mean it like that, I swear! It's just no one—well, we've never really hung out together."

"We used to. A little bit at least."

"That was five years ago."

Avery wanted to say something meaningful, but all she could come up with was that she didn't have other friends either. As weird as it had been for Fletcher to want to talk to her after the incident, she found herself wanting to talk with him. He was nice. He understood her. He knew what it was like to have awful, haunting memories that never really left you.

She shrugged.

"There's nothing to do down here. Wanna go upstairs?"

Avery had never really been in a boy's room before. *But it's Fletch*, she told herself. *No big deal.* "Cool."

"I'm glad you stopped by. My brain is kind of crazy." He drew a circle around his temple with his finger.

"Believe me, I know the feeling."

Fletcher opened the door to his bedroom. Avery didn't know what she was expecting, but it was pretty normal: bed with navy-blue sheets. Desk with nothing on it. Alarm clock in the corner. It didn't look quite as sparse as the rest of the house, but it still had that uncomfortable feeling that someone might have stayed there but no one really lived there.

Avery took a seat at the desk while Fletcher sank onto his bed, balancing his water bottle in his lap. His gaze connected with hers, and Avery realized she had never noticed how unusual his eyes were. They were a brown so golden and pale it bordered on amber.

"Is it just about what happened to your mom?" Fletcher asked.

"That makes me feel crazy?" Avery shook her head. "It's a combination of things. My mom's death, my preoccupied dad, being the daughter of the chief of police." She stopped, licked her lips, and smiled. "Am I boring you yet?"

"No," he said, wrapping his arms around his shins. "Not at all. I feel the same way. Sometimes my mind is all jumbled up but lately... I mean, after"—he rolled his eyes—"all this, it feels worse."

"Yeah."

• • •

Fletcher felt his pulse start to speed up. He wanted to talk to her. He wanted to tell her everything.

Everything that I think *happened.*

Fletcher was trying to stay calm. Avery's expression was hard to read, somewhere between blank neutrality and stark judgment.

"Do you remember everything about what happened?" he asked. "Are there gaps in your memory?"

"Gaps? Yeah, Fletch, we talked about this. The blackouts and—"

"No..."—he swung his head—"not just blackouts. Even now. There are...blank spaces. Missing pieces. Like, you remember the walkway that leads to the door and you remember being in the house, but you can't remember how you got in."

Avery looked confused and Fletcher barreled on. "Like, was the door unlocked? Did you just walk in, or did you have a key? Did someone let you in?"

"I guess, but I don't think I forget anything really important..."

Fletcher grabbed Avery's hand. "But what if what was missing was the *most* important thing?"

There was a flash of panic in Avery's eyes.

"What if what I can't remember is—" He looked down at his own hands and let Avery go as if she'd burned him. "Never mind."

"No, Fletch, I get it. I do. You think that if you could fill in those gaps, you could help find the killer."

Fletcher stared at Avery for a long, hard moment. With her chin slightly hitched, her hair curling at her shoulders, she looked so innocent, almost angelic, like one of those marble statues in the cemetery. He could trust her. He could tell her.

"Fletch? Fletcher, honey, are you home?" His mother's voice trailed from downstairs. He wondered if Avery could also feel the change in the air between them.

"I'm here, Mom. Avery's with me."

"Come on down, please. Both of you," she replied.

Avery cleared her throat, her voice a hoarse whisper. "Are we in trouble?"

Fletcher gave a noncommittal shrug and stood. "You should probably go."

She nodded and followed Fletcher down the stairs, smiling at Mrs. Carroll on the landing. "Hello, Mrs. Carroll. I was just—" Avery looked from Mrs. Carroll to Fletcher and back again. "I was just dropping off some homework for Fletcher." She snatched up her backpack. "I should go."

Mrs. Carroll's eyes didn't leave her son's face. "That's probably a good idea. Do you need a ride?"

"No, thank you." Avery stuck her thumb over her shoulder. "I live super close."

• • •

"Thanks a lot, Mom." Fletcher snorted. "Kick out the one person who doesn't think I'm a complete socio." He'd adopted the moniker they had used at school when he passed by.

"You are not a sociopath."

"Whatever. I don't care what they think. I care what Avery thinks." The reality of what he had said hit him squarely in the chest. Did he really care what Avery thought about him?

"Fletcher, you know it's not a good time for you to get too wrapped up in your friends. Especially a girl like Avery Templeton."

"What's that supposed to mean? I've known Avery since we moved here. She's the only kid who's ever been nice to me except for Adam. What do you have against her?"

His mother wouldn't meet his eyes. "It's just not a great idea right now. You need to distance yourself from everything that happened in the woods. And frankly, Avery is a big part of that. I'm just thinking about you, honey." She brushed the side of his face tenderly. "I want you to be okay. Dr. Palmer is going to see you tomorrow afternoon, and he and I think—"

Again, Fletcher shrugged off his mother and her concern. "I'm fine, Mom. You have no idea what I need."

• • •

Avery peeled the crusts off her sandwich, piling them at the side of her plate.

Chief Templeton gestured at the discards. "Dinner not to your liking, Princess Avy?"

She overlooked his barb. "Do you like Mrs. Carroll, Dad?"

"Mrs. Carroll? Sure, why not?" He paused and narrowed his eyes. "Wait, this isn't a fix-up, right? You're not trying to—"

Avery shrugged and picked up her sandwich. "She's super-protective of Fletch. A million more times than normal."

"Her son was beaten to within an inch of his life, Avy. I think a little overprotection is warranted."

"I don't know. It's more than that. I was over there today, and we were up in Fletch's room when she came home—"

Chief Templeton held up a silencing hand, his eyebrow arching. "You were in a boy's room without any parents in the house?"

Avery rolled her eyes. "It's Fletch, Dad. Get a grip."

The chief gave her a stern look. "'Get a grip'? Did you really just tell me to 'get a grip'?"

Normally, Avery would have flushed red to the scalp and waited for her father to read her the riot act, but this was bigger than a conversation about boys.

"I really think there's something wrong with her. I think maybe she could have had something to do with what happened."

The chief closed his mouth, then pointed a finger at his daughter before starting in. "First of all, you're not out of the hole for shooting off your mouth. Second of all, are you really accusing a mother of killing her son's friend and beating her own child to cover it up?"

"Fletcher can't remember the face of his attacker. What if it's because his brain can't handle it? What if his brain is trying to protect him from knowing that his mother is a murderer?"

"Motive?"

Avery bit her lip. "None, but—"

"This conversation is over, Avery. Go to your room."

Avery gaped, feeling betrayed. "I was just thinking out loud."

"First you were 'just in a fight,' then you were just shooting off your mouth. Now you're 'just thinking.' You're like a different kid lately, Avy, and frankly, one I don't like very much. Your mother and I raised you to behave better than this."

Her father's soft, gray-blue eyes had turned cold and hard. His jaw was set and Avery could see the pulse of his muscle along his jawbone. Avery's eyes started to burn, her lower lip trembling.

"I just want to help my friend."

"And I want you to be the kid you were two weeks ago. We can't always get what we want. Now go to your room."

Avery stomped up the stairs, unsure whether she was hurt or angry or both. Her father had always been on her side and would always listen to her theories on cases, no matter how far-fetched.

You're like a different kid…

She slammed her bedroom door.

And frankly, one I don't think I like very much.

TWENTY-TWO

The next day, Fletcher waited for Avery at her locker. There were the usual after-school sounds: people talking, papers shuffling, lockers slamming. But every few seconds he heard it—"socio" coughed into someone's hand, followed by tittering laughter.

Socio, murderer, killer—Dr. Palmer said that Fletcher couldn't control other people's perceptions of him so he should let those remarks roll off his back. What Fletcher *could* control, according to his shrink, was how he let others make him feel. And he wasn't supposed to let their nasty comments bother him. But he couldn't shake off the stares.

He was going to tell Avery how one of the memories had clicked into place last night, like one of those games where the squares drop down to plug up the empty holes.

He remembered Adam beckoning him over, and the two of them standing at the edge of a wide gully. Adam was pointing to a crisscross of bleached, white bones.

The memory made all the hairs on the back of Fletcher's neck stand up.

"Whose bones do you suppose...?"

The voice was indistinct—either Adam's or Fletcher's and foggy, just like the rest of what he remembered from that afternoon.

But what happened next? Who else was there?

"Hey, Fletch."

Avery looked cute in her enormous sweatshirt. Her light-brown hair spilling out of the hood, which hung down her back. She smiled.

Fletcher smiled back. "Hey. Got a second?"

• • •

They slid to sit across from each other at a picnic table at the back of the school. Fletcher seemed distracted when they sat down, and Avery really wanted to tell him to get on with it. The wooden bench was only semi-dry, and the moisture was seeping into her jeans and making her shiver.

Fletcher gnawed his lower lip, then swatted at his ear like there was a gnat.

"You okay?" she asked.

He blinked at her, as though just realizing she was there.

• • •

He started to sweat. His stomach started to roil.

Tell her about the dream.

Tell her about the whispers.

Tell her...

Fletcher pressed his lips together in a thin line. "Have you ever...have you ever felt like your brain was full?"

Avery rolled her eyes. "Every time I'm in calculus. I swear if

Mrs. Stevens gives us one more set of equations, my head is going to explode." She puffed up her cheeks and pantomimed her head exploding, then grinned at him—one of those wide, carefree grins of hers that he loved.

"Not like that. Not exactly. Do you ever feel like, maybe, something's taking over your mind?"

The look on Avery's face cut him like a knife. Her eyes clouded and the smile dropped from her lips. She paled, and he knew she was thinking about her mother.

"I'm sorry," he said quickly.

"No, no." Avery shook her head, pushing a clump of hair behind her ear. "That's all right." She smiled, but this time it didn't look authentic. "Have I ever had my thoughts hijacked? Yeah. Haven't you?"

Shock waves, like tiny pinpricks, burned all over him. She understood.

Then she continued, "Like when I'm supposed to be studying and all I can think about is a cheeseburger? Or when I'm super tired, but my mind is wide-awake thinking about stuff?"

Fletcher's twinge of joy faded. He swallowed. "Have they ever been hijacked by something darker?"

Avery blinked. "By a bad memory?"

He nodded.

"Yeah. Sometimes I want to think of my mom in a good way, but I keep picturing her in the accident instead. But that's normal, right?"

Fletcher realized she was waiting for his approval, so he pumped his head. "Sure. Yeah."

"Do you think about Adam that way sometimes?"

He looked away, worrying his bottom lip. The errant thoughts of Adam weren't what scared him. It was more than that. The whispers started small—a *psst*, a huff—and swelled to a chorus of voices that he couldn't ignore.

"Sometimes I hear things."

Avery didn't laugh or call him crazy. "Things like what?"

Voices. "I don't know. Just…"

"Well, I know when my dad got whacked in the head this one time, he complained of ringing in his ears for months." She licked her lips, started to smile again. "He kept telling me to 'Turn down whatever is making that stupid noise!'" She started to laugh. "I had no idea what he was talking about, and he wouldn't admit that he was hearing things." Fletcher forced himself to join her laughter.

"Yeah," he lied. "That's it. I guess it's normal."

"Normal is a setting on a dryer," Avery said, suddenly more serious. "I saw it on a magnet once. But I like what it means—there is no normal. We are all a little off, and that's okay." She looked so sure that Fletcher wanted to believe her. Maybe he *was* just a different kind of normal.

Though the voices in his head didn't quite agree.

• • •

That night, Fletcher tried to stay awake. Every time he nodded off, he fell into the same weird dream. In it, he was in the bathroom at his old house. There was nothing quirky or dreamlike about the setting—it was the same old bathroom with the same old white subway tiles and Susan's same collection of shampoo bottles and hair-care products taking up every inch of space.

In Fletcher's dream, he watched himself push the door closed so that he was alone. His reflection appeared in the mirror on the medicine cabinet. It was him, his face a little more filled out and his hair longer and curlier.

It was not just one reflection though. Like a fun-house mirror, it was him and him again, a collection of Fletchers.

The first Fletcher turned on the tap, leaned forward, and splashed water on his face. When he straightened to look at his reflections, none of the other Fletchers moved. They all just looked curiously at the original Fletcher. They were staring because the water from the tap wasn't water at all. It was blood. And it was smeared across his cheeks, little droplets hanging from his eyelashes and dripping toward his chin.

This was the point at which Fletcher always woke with a start, the smell of blood clogging his nostrils.

He was in the middle of the dream yet again when, this time, the mirror crashed. It sounded like a sonic boom, so loud that it rattled his teeth and made him sit bolt upright in his bed.

"Did you hear that?" his mother asked. She was in his doorway, in her bathrobe, one hand pulling the collar tight against her throat. When she clicked on his bedside lamp, Fletcher could see the hollows in her cheeks and the bags underneath her eyes. She wasn't sleeping well either.

Fletcher raked a hand through his damp hair. "I thought I was dreaming."

"No, I heard something crash."

He kicked off the covers and pressed his bare feet onto the floor. "I'll go check it out."

"Fletcher, no." It was a halfhearted attempt to stop him. Fletcher could barely feel his mother's fingertips brush against the fabric of his T-shirt. "It sounded like it came from downstairs."

There was another unmistakable crash and then the squeal of tires.

A dog barked.

A light flicked on at the neighbor's house.

Fletcher ran down the stairs and yanked open the front door, peering down the walk. His mother turned on the porch light.

The driveway and grass looked like a battlefield of oozing yolks and little broken shells. But it wasn't the egging that had woken Fletcher and his mother.

Fletcher walked down the driveway, careful not to slip on the egg slime, and stopped beside his car. He gently fingered what remained of the splintered back window of his Toyota Celica.

"Oh, son, I'm so sorry. I heard all the commotion." It was Mr. Henderson from across the street. The old man was in his slippers and robe. "Kids can be such jackasses. I can help you call the insurance company in the morning. We should file a police report too."

Fletcher nodded. On the edge of his vision, he watched his mother gingerly step down the walk, take one look at the debris on the ground and the damage to Fletcher's car, and turn back to the house—probably hoping that Fletcher wouldn't see her shoulders shaking as she cried.

Fletcher glanced into the car. He put his hand through the open space on the back window and fished through the glittering glass. A rock, about the size of a tennis ball but slightly more compact. He picked it up, feeling the heft of it in his palm and swallowing hard at the words scrawled across it: ADAM DIDN'T DESERVE 2DIE. U DO.

He looked out to the street and launched the rock as far as he could.

• • •

By the time Avery got to homeroom, everyone was already seated. The murmur in the halls was better than any announcement, so the whole school already knew that someone had vandalized Fletcher's house the night before.

Avery was upset. She had called Fletcher three times that morning, but he hadn't answered either his cell or the home phone, and he hadn't called her back. She texted, **Are you okay?** just before she'd walked onto the school grounds that morning, but still nothing.

"I heard it was all over the house, all over everything—eggs, shaving cream, the works." Kaylee looked almost pleased with her replay of the events at Fletcher's house.

Avery shook her head. "That's awful. Fletcher has gone through enough."

"Fletcher?" Kaylee stood up, nearly nose to nose with Avery. "He seems pretty fine to me. I mean, he's alive."

"God, Kaylee! He's totally traumatized. He watched his best friend die! And now people…"—Avery looked around, eyes narrowed and accusatory—"*you* people are accusing him of murder. He's our friend! We've known him since he was kid!"

"No," Tim said, standing up. "We've only known Fletch for a few years. We knew Adam since he was a kid. And Fletcher has never wanted to be anyone's friend. He barely even talks to anyone."

"You know an awful lot about Fletch, Avery. Maybe you're so defensive of him because you like him." Kaylee flicked her glossy hair. "Maybe you're defending him because you know that Fletcher didn't do this alone."

Avery gasped. "What are you talking about?"

The kids around them exchanged looks, and a surprised murmur rippled through the room.

Tim shot Kaylee a look. "Come on, that's not fair. Don't drag Avery into this."

Kaylee cocked a hip, clearly not ready to back down. "I didn't drag Avery anywhere—she did this to herself. Think about it. She was the one who found Fletcher."

"I was on a search team."

Kaylee shrugged. "So was I, but I didn't find him. You told us not to leave the group for any reason, Avery, but who left the group? You. And when you did, you went straight to Fletcher. Coincidence?" Her blond eyebrows rose.

Avery wanted to defend herself, but her voice was trapped in her chest. She looked around for someone to defend her, for a teacher to step in, but she was surrounded by suspicious stares. "That's not true."

"And then the only person Fletcher wanted to talk to in the hospital? Avery again." Kaylee was gathering steam now, patrolling the classroom like a prosecutor in front of an adoring court. "Everyone knows Fletcher was jealous of Adam. Fletcher's a freak. Adam was perfect. He practically had a full-ride college scholarship already, a brand-new car…he had everything. Fletcher had nothing, and he couldn't take it anymore."

"That's not—"Avery tried to interrupt.

"Kaylee," Tim said again.

"And everyone knows you had a major crush on Adam. You probably just got mad because you knew it would never happen for you and him. One of those scorned-lover things. 'If I can't have him, no one can.'"

Avery's head started to spin. The only thing she could register was Kaylee's sharp, snotty voice.

"He thought you were a freak too." Kaylee pointed her index finger, jabbing at the air in front of Avery's chest.

"He didn't—" Avery heard herself say. "Adam and I were friends."

"No you weren't. When was the last time he even talked to you? When was the last time he said anything more than 'Excuse me' or 'Can I borrow a pencil?' He felt sorry for you because your mom died. Just like Fletcher: You. Are. A. Freak." She punctuated each word so that they hit Avery like poisoned darts. "You probably wanted him dead."

"What's going on in here?" Ms. Holly broke through the door like a wave of fresh air, and Avery felt her legs nearly give way. She wanted to report Kaylee, to defend herself and Fletcher, but there was nothing left in her. Kaylee had shredded her, and Avery didn't know how to begin to put herself back together.

The class answered Ms. Holly with silence. No one stepped in. No one pointed out that what Kaylee had said was mean and just plain wrong from beginning to end. No one asked about Avery.

"Take your seats, everyone. Come on, come on. Class is starting."

Avery could hear Ms. Holly's voice, but it felt like her ears were full of cotton.

"Avery? You can sit down now."

Avery snapped to attention, gasping for breath as though she had been holding it the whole time. Tim wouldn't meet her eyes. Kaylee looked unaffected, lazily flipping through pages in her textbook. Avery sank into her seat. *Did that really just happen?*

TWENTY-THREE

Avery had no idea how she made it through the rest of her classes. Around her, the rumors circulated—that she and Fletcher had attacked Adam together, that it was their plot all along, that they were the modern-day murderous Bonnie and Clyde.

"She snapped," Avery heard someone say under her breath.

"Fletcher is in love with Avery. He'd do anything she said…"

"Avery said if he got rid of Adam…"

Each new theory was a stab to Avery's self-worth, but the accusatory stares were even worse. Once upon a time, she had been invisible, a goody-goody—now she was a celebrity criminal, tried and convicted in front of a jury of her peers. There was no reason to defend herself. The decision had already been made: Fletcher killed Adam, and Avery had helped. Maybe Fletcher would have defended her, but he didn't show up at school nor did he answer any of Avery's calls or texts. When the final bell rang, she tried again.

After the third ring, a woman answered in an uncertain, scared voice. "Hello?"

"Mrs. Carroll?"

"Who is this, please?"

Avery cleared her throat. "It's Avery. Avery Templeton. I'm a friend of Fletcher's." She knew that Mrs. Carroll knew exactly who she was, but adding that she was Fletcher's friend somehow felt important.

"Yes, Avery. May I help you?"

Avery's eyes started to fill with tears, even though she knew the offer to help was part of a greeting rather than any actual offer. She couldn't talk to her father much, and she'd always been able to talk with her mother…

She cleared her throat. "Is Fletcher there?"

There was an extra-long silence. "I'm sorry. Fletcher can't come to the phone right now."

Avery found herself nodding even though she knew Mrs. Carroll couldn't see her. "Sure, yeah, okay. Would it be okay if I came by the house later?"

Another pause. "I don't think so, Avery."

"Can you tell Fletcher that I called? I've been trying to get hold—"

"Sure, Avery," Mrs. Carroll's soft voice cut her off smoothly. "I'll let him know that you were looking for him."

Avery was about to reply when the line dropped and she was listening to silence. She stared at her phone as if that would explain everything: Fletcher seemingly avoiding her and Mrs. Carroll's quick cutoff. Or did Mrs. Carroll just not want her to talk to Fletcher?

Avery turned and Ellison, standing with Tim and some other kids, wandered over to her. "Hey," Ellison said.

Avery wasn't in the mood to talk, her head swimming with thoughts about Fletch and Mrs. Carroll. "Hey," she said offhandedly.

"About all the stuff—all the rumors and stuff—"

Avery stiffened, nearly ready to sprint for the car the second she heard her father honk. "I've gotta go." She turned her back on Ellison, trying hard not to strain to hear the murmuring voices behind her.

"That was fast," Chief Templeton said. "Didn't you want to say good-bye to your friends?"

What friends? Avery thought. Instead, she just shook her head, eyes focused on her hands resting on her jeans. "Can we just go?"

They drove in silence for a few moments. Then her father started to make small talk—something about a cake coming into the office, the sugar rush killing a week of "clean eating."

"They think that I had something to do with it," Avery said finally.

"What's that?

She couldn't announce—admit—it again.

"Nothing. Have you heard anything from the Carrolls? Fletcher wasn't in school again today. Did any of the tox or blood screens come back?"

Chief Templeton rolled the car to a stop at a red light, and Avery could see the muscle jump along his jawline. "We're not going to talk about this anymore, Avery."

She crossed her arms in front of her chest, the needling pain she'd been feeling all day replaced by an indignant anger.

"You shouldn't have to worry about stuff like this. You're just a kid."

"Just a kid? Dad, my friend died. And my other friend is being accused of his murder."

"No one is accusing Fletcher of murder."

"No one but the whole school."

"We're not talking about this. You're too close to this case—I shouldn't have even talked to you about it in the first place."

"Dad, I was the one who found Fletcher, remember?"

"Yes, Avery, I remember. But it's time to let me take over, okay? We're doing what we can."

"What you *can*?" Avery spat out. "You're letting the entire town prosecute Fletch and his mom. His locker and his house have been vandalized, and you're just letting it happen!"

"We are taking care of it. Just because you can't see the progress we've made right in front of you doesn't mean that we haven't been building a case."

"What kind of progress? And a case against who? I mean, someone tried to kill me, Dad. Has that figured into your investigation? Or are you just brushing that aside because you also think Fletch is guilty?"

"I'm not going to come down on you for being so disrespectful because I know you're hurting right now. But, Avery, you'd better watch your mouth."

"Dad!"

"This is out of your hands, out of your life now, kid."

Avery was seething. She glanced over at her dad whose face looked almost serene, like the last three minutes had never happened. She hated how he did that, went from animated one minute to shut down the next. She wondered what else he was able to hide with that closed-off look.

• • •

Fletcher overheard his mother's exchange with Avery. He turned his back to the door, and a few minutes later, his mother knocked on his door frame.

"Anyone call for me?"

"No, honey."

He didn't have to turn around to know that his mother was holding a plate in one hand and a glass of milk in the other. He didn't have to turn around to know that she was feeding him those pills again, the ones from Dr. Palmer or Dr. Roy or maybe some other doctor who she had dreamed up to poke at him and shine lights in his eyes even before all of this happened.

"I don't want anything to eat."

"You have to eat something, Fletcher."

He hated the patronizing way she said his name. Her sigh told him she was tired of being his mother, his warden, his gatekeeper.

"Just leave me alone."

Fletcher heard her put the plate and milk down on his desk. He knew she wouldn't leave without poking at him, asking him questions, and trying to get him to talk.

"How are the blackouts?"

The blackouts were shorter now, sharp pieces of dark. But some of the time from his escape was starting to fade into a gray fog. He could see shadows and shapes. He could hear voices.

Maybe he could piece it all together. Maybe if he really concentrated…

"Try not to stress yourself. Remember what the doctor said?"

He didn't.

"Just relax and make sure you eat your sandwich and finish your milk."

He stayed quiet.

"Fletcher?" Her voice rose.

"Sure, Mom."

• • •

Avery and her father didn't speak until they turned down her street. "So I'm just going to drop you off and go back to the station. I shouldn't be too late tonight. Maybe we can go out, grab a couple of burgers?"

He poked her on the shoulder when Avery didn't respond. "Avy?"

"Burgers. Sure, fine, whatever."

The chief guided the car down the street and into their long driveway, the tires grating as they bit the gravel. He pushed the car into park and turned toward her.

"What else is going on, Avy? Come on, something with school? Boys?"

Avery tried to hide the scowl on her face.

"You know you can talk to me about anything."

Avery got out of the car. She kicked the door of the police cruiser shut. "Right, Dad. Anything except for police work."

Chief Templeton rolled down his window. "That's not fair, Avy. This is police business." The stern look in his eyes shifted, and suddenly the chief was her father once again. "A kid is dead. And I don't want you messed up in this. I won't put you in any danger. I don't know what I'd do if I lost you too."

A lump formed in the back of her throat, and Avery was pulled back to the months after her mother passed. The casserole brigade had stopped coming, the "just checking in" calls had gone silent. For the rest of the community, life went back to business as usual. And they expected Avery and her father to do the same. But there was nothing usual about their new existence. She and her dad had tried to do everything the same way—church on Sundays, dinner at the table from serving dishes and plates—but the silence was too hard.

Avery and her father found there was safety in the darkness, in meals eaten off paper towels in front of the kitchen sink or in front of the TV, the flickering light an appreciated shadow for the tears in her father's eyes.

Avery softened. "You won't lose me, Dad. I'm not stupid." She offered a small smile. "I am your daughter after all."

The chief smiled back. "I'm not sure that makes either of us exempt from stupidity."

Avery jammed her hands into the pockets of her jeans. "I just want to help, that's all. I know Fletcher. I knew Adam. Just let me help."

Her father let out a measured sigh. "I'll tell you what. You can help from in there." He pointed to the house. "No crime-scene visiting. No interrogation, and definitely no strip searches."

"Ew! Dad! Gross!"

"In the house, Avy."

"Will you at least tell me what you find and then listen to my theory?"

"I'll tell you what. If your homework is done and the house is cleaned, I'll let you know what we've got and listen to your theory."

"Homework *and* housework?"

"A cornerstone of a good investigation is an impeccable police report."

"And housework?"

Chief Templeton shrugged and clicked the key in the ignition, letting the cruiser's engine roar to life. "Hey, the chief of police likes a clean house. Do we have a deal?"

Avery smiled in spite of her dad's annoying rules. "Fine!" She trudged to the front porch and spun around, pointing at her father. "But don't forget, we have a deal!"

Chief Templeton waved, waiting until Avery was in the house with enough time to bolt the lock before he pulled out of the driveway.

• • •

Avery finished all of her homework and nearly wore out the battery on her cell phone playing games before she groaned and texted her father. It was only four forty, but she was starving.

ETA? She texted.

7…ISH was the response.

Avery groaned and tried another fruitless call to Fletcher's cell, which went directly to voice mail. She bopped her phone against her side and thought about school, about hateful, snotty Kaylee's face.

She knew Fletch had nothing to do with hurting Adam. She knew she certainly didn't either.

"Screw this," she said, sliding her phone into her back pocket. "If Fletch doesn't want to clear his name and Dad doesn't want to clear Fletch's name, then I will."

She took the stairs two at a time, cast a sideways look at her munched-up bike, then hopped onto her father's, pedaling hard once she hit the street.

Adam's house was in the same neighborhood as Avery's and Fletcher's, just set back a little farther at the edge of the woods. She glanced at her phone when she reached Adam's house. The flickering "Low Battery" readout popped up first, right above the time—5:17.

She had no idea what she would tell Adam's mother when she opened the door. *I'll just tell her that I let Adam borrow a book or something in homeroom... Maybe I could just...*

Avery rang the bell before she realized how stupid her plan was. What mother was going to let Avery paw through her dead son's stuff? She was about to turn and leave when the garage door startled her. She hugged the outside wall and watched Mrs. Marshall's blue Volvo back out slowly.

Avery stared, hidden behind a decorative, swirly pine tree. She watched Mrs. Marshall pause before turning her car around and zipping for the mouth of the street. Avery dove underneath the garage door just before it closed.

* * *

Fletcher hated when his mom talked about him like he wasn't even there. She was on the phone with Dr. Palmer, who didn't have a free appointment until the end of the week, saying things like she was "concerned" and that Fletcher "seemed upset" while he sat fifteen feet away.

She could have been talking to him. She *should* have been. Fletcher knew how Dr. Palmer would respond. It would be something about compartmentalizing trauma and creating a stable environment. Consistent and comfortable.

He looked around the sparse house. "Consistent and comfortable" wasn't how he would describe it at all. His mother was always nervously flittering around, and even though they had been there for five years, it had never felt like home. There were no pictures on the walls, no family heirlooms, no backyard graveyard of old bicycles. His father wasn't at this house, and neither was his older sister, Susan.

Fletcher bit his lip.

He knew that his dad's and Susan's absences had nothing to do with the half-empty house. He knew it was because of him. That was another memory he didn't want to revisit: the way blood poured over Susan's lips, their mother in between them, her hands glossy and red.

Fletcher had wondered then what was wrong with him.

Now, though the bandage was off and his stitches were out, his head still throbbed. The doctors at Dan River Falls Community Hospital had said there would be no lasting damage, but Fletcher didn't believe them. Otherwise why wouldn't his memories be coming back to him? They weren't becoming clearer as time wore on. If anything, the events of that day were getting darker, grainier, and grittier.

Fletcher glanced at his mother who had turned her back, her voice dropping to a low murmur as she spoke to Dr. Palmer.

He knew. His mother was making plans to send him away. He felt as if the bare walls of this stupid house were closing in.

His heart smacked against his rib cage. His breath was coming in tight, shallow puffs. It was getting harder to breathe.

He had to get away.

He had to escape the doctors who were coming for him.

They would surely arrive any minute. They thought he was crazy, those doctors in their white coats. They were going to prod at his brain and *make* him remember. He didn't want that.

How could his mother betray him? She was practically begging them to take him away. She looked over her shoulder, then looked away, obviously ashamed at being caught.

There was no time. Fletcher would have to go now, right now, if he wanted to escape. If he wanted to be free, he couldn't be at home when the doctors came. And he had to find out who had killed Adam. He had to do it now.

TWENTY-FOUR

The light in Adam's garage clicked off after the door shut. Avery stood up, her eyes adjusting to the darkness.

The two-car garage was empty, but the walls were lined with shelving and all manner of storage boxes and sporting goods— canoes, a sled, a hockey stick, a soccer goal. Adam had been naturally athletic. Avery swallowed back a lump and went to the door.

It was open.

She stepped into the Marshalls' living room.

The enormous room was lined with windows overlooking a huge deck that opened onto dense forest. Avery tiptoed through the room, taking in the lush beige-and-white furnishings. Everything matched. She picked her way through the living room and kitchen, then climbed the carpeted stairs, peeking in rooms until she found the one that had to be Adam's.

She recognized his backpack next to the desk, but it was like looking at a magazine photo, not a teen boy's room. Everything looked posed. Stacks of books were arranged by size on the desk, and the bed was made so tightly it looked like no one had ever slept there. It was the kind of room that every parent wanted, but no kid would want to live in.

"Okay, now to find a motive," she whispered to herself. "Maybe Adam was in some kind of trouble? Maybe someone was mad at him…"

She slowly pulled open his top desk drawer, surprised that everything inside was placed just as precisely as everything on top of the desk.

Avery thought of her own room, which was a psychedelic mess of creativity and frustration that resulted in piles of cast-off clothing, books, and nice shoes tossed over in favor of sneakers.

She pushed aside the notebooks and frowned at a wide, flat box. Popping it open, she startled at the contents—a series of knives, arranged smallest to largest, each equidistant from the next. Except for one. Avery fingered the velvet between a short, orange-handled hunting knife and a longer Bowie-type knife.

Avery was vaguely familiar with the rest of the knives in the collection—a simple penknife, a pocketknife with a burnished leather–looking handle and glossy brass studs, and a small dagger with a carved dragon handle, the reptile's eye a sparkling red jewel.

Each knife was clean and looked unused, polished even.

Was Adam a collector?

Avery had no idea what Adam's hobbies were, other than sports and Kaylee, but seemingly knife collecting—and an obsessive-compulsive bent toward organization—were important to him. She snapped a picture of the box and carefully put it back in the drawer, pawing through the next two and finding nothing of note.

She went to his closet. His clothes hung in groupings by color and style—long sleeves with long sleeves, collars all facing the same way. The militaristic organization reminded her of her father's closet.

She fingered a row of soft flannels and dug through the pockets of his jackets, hoping to find the missing knife.

What if he took it hiking with him?

Her father had never mentioned finding any weapons—but then again, she thought angrily, he probably wouldn't. *If Adam had taken the knife, why hadn't he used it to defend himself?*

She went through his bureau, poking through the neat stacks of clothing until she got to the bottom drawer. It opened slowly, the top of the drawer hissing over the thick stack of sweatshirts folded inside. Avery ran her fingers over them, then dipped to the bottom of the drawer, her fingertips landing on something papery.

She pulled out a stack of hundred-dollar bills.

Eleven of them, clipped with a paper clip and organized exactly as Avery would expect: each facing the same way, edges squared, a perfect rectangular stack. She carefully pulled out the sweatshirts and stared—the bottom of the drawer was lined with stacks of bills. There was a thick stack of twenties and another of tens. Avery was too scared to count them. She snapped a picture with her phone and frowned when the screen went black. Her battery was dead.

A rumble came from downstairs. *The garage door!* She ran to the window, ducking low, hoping against hope that she was imagining the sound. But the dark blue Volvo was pulling up the driveway.

• • •

Fletcher slipped out his front door. He was so jittery that his hands and feet felt tingly.

They're not going to get me. They're not going to get me.

He clenched his fists and started to run. The sound of his regular footfalls reassured him.

"Adam," he whispered out loud to himself. "I have to find Adam."

Maybe Adam wasn't really dead. Maybe this was all some big, horrible joke. The thought made Fletcher feel better. Maybe this was all just some elaborate prank.

He still needed to find out what happened to Adam. If he did, then the police wouldn't arrest him, and the doctors wouldn't restrain him and shoot him up with drugs. He had to act quickly.

Run, run!

What was that? Who was that?

It wasn't his fault—his mother, she had—

Put your head down and keep running. Keep running, Fletch.

I had to protect him. I was protecting him.

What the hell are you doing?

Pain arced through his skull. It throbbed behind his eyes. He kept running.

She wasn't there—it wasn't her—

Don't ever stop. I can't ever stop.

I didn't mean to. I didn't mean to. Oh God. Oh God, please, no, I didn't mean to.

Footsteps pounding. A ragged, metered breath. Sweat at his temples. The edges of his lips cracked and bone dry.

"I'm going to give you something to make you feel better," Dr. Palmer had said. "Something to maybe make you think a little more clearly."

He'd felt the doctor tug the sleeve of his shirt up. The cold bite of an alcohol-soaked cotton ball had swabbed his arm. He'd felt a prick in his shoulder. Then everything had gone dark.

"Fletcher? Fletcher, can you hear me? It's Dr. Palmer. You're safe. We're friends. Can you tell me again what you remember?"

Fletcher stopped on the sidewalk when the images—memories, thoughts, whatever the hell they were—kept coming. He pinched his eyes shut and willed them to go away, then slammed his palm to the side of his head, trying to shake them out.

"Something's taking over my brain." He whispered it like a mantra. "Something's taking over my brain."

He was walking at a quick, clipped pace, unsure of where he was headed. He stopped and stared when the sidewalk abruptly ended.

He was in a cul-de-sac. Fletcher was in front of Adam's house.

He heard the rumble of a car engine. It was Mrs. Marshall's midnight-colored Volvo. He instinctively crouched behind a bush.

He watched her back out and then was compelled to go forward, his sneakers crunching on the gravel driveway. The house looked mostly dark. But a flicker of movement caught his eye. A dark figure slowly edging open the door of one of the bedrooms.

Fletcher squinted. The door that opened was in Adam's room.

Whoever was walking around inside was drenched in shadows and moving slowly, carefully, pausing every few steps to cock his head and listen. Fletcher held his breath. *Who would be in Adam's room?*

Adam was a middle child, with a college-age brother and a little sister still in grade school. Fletcher remembered Adam saying his dad traveled a lot.

Was there a prowler in Adam's house?

He thought of the rocks hurling through his windows, the eggs, the graffiti, the searing notes in his locker and mailbox. Surely no one would do that to Adam's family. He considered knocking or trying the door but dismissed the idea. If the person in Adam's room was a cousin or a friend, what was he supposed to say? "Hey, I'm the kid the whole town thinks is a killer, and I thought it would be cool to drop in and say hey…"

He cut his eyes to Adam's window again and the figure was gone. Had he imagined it?

No.

Another flash of movement.

Fletcher stayed close to the tree line, advancing toward the house. He still hadn't worked out a plan to get inside when he heard the hum of an engine moving closer. Then the nip of headlights cutting through the dim twilight. He glanced over his shoulder at the dark blue Volvo and broke into a run, breath ripping through his lungs, sweat beading down his rib cage.

He zipped across the front yard and bolted down the side of the house, hoping for a cut through to a side street or a thickened clump of trees. What he heard was a window scraping open and the scuffling of feet down wood siding—before the person attached to the scuffling feet landed right on top of him.

"What the—" He landed facedown on the moist grass, the breath sucked from his lungs.

It's happening again, it's happening again…

An immovable weight against his chest. His arms and legs pinned. His whole body useless, betraying his brain, synapses telling him to move. Then the surge of strength that came from somewhere, that promised to make everything okay.

• • •

The first wallop caught Avery between the eyes. White-hot needles of pain sparked out across her forehead, and she pressed her face into her hands, sure she would only feel mealy mash where her skull had once been.

"*Owww!*"

Another bash, this one to the back of her head. This one far less painful because her thick ponytail took most of the blow.

"Avery?" Fletcher's voice was veiled in shock and horror.

Avery moved her hands so she could open an eye.

"What are you kids doing?"

Avery and Fletcher startled at the shrill tone of Mrs. Marshall's voice. Her eyes, ice blue and piercing like Adam's had been, darted from Fletcher to Avery and back again as she stood over them, cell phone clutched in one hand.

"What are you kids doing here?" she snapped again.

Avery and Fletcher looked at each other, dumbfounded. Avery

had no idea why Fletcher was at the Marshalls, and she prayed that he wouldn't tell Mrs. Marshall that she'd been inside the house.

Fletcher started speaking first, winding the lie as he went. "I was just out walking—jogging—and I…" He shot a glance at Avery. "I saw Avery, and I guess I scared her because she took off running."

The hard look on Mrs. Marshall's face didn't change. She looked at Avery. "Avery?"

Avery cleared her throat, hoping some miraculous story would tumble out.

"I knew Avery was coming over to give her condolences," Fletcher said carefully, his eyes never leaving Avery's. "I thought I might catch her so we could do it together, but like I said, I guess I surprised her."

Avery nodded, relief flooding over her. "I wanted to see how you and your family were doing," she said, the lie bitter on her tongue. "I wanted to tell you how sorry I was for your loss. You weren't home, and then I ran into Fletcher. I got startled, I guess." She pulled her feet up and dusted off her pants, shoving herself off the grass. "I'm really sorry to have disturbed you."

Mrs. Marshall's demeanor seemed to soften, her blue eyes going glossy. "You both surprised me. That's all." She glanced down at the phone in her hand. "Sorry, we're all very jumpy." She shot a quick glance to Fletcher. "As you can understand."

It was then that Avery realized Mrs. Marshall had never actually looked at Fletcher. Sure, she had glanced at him for a beat but her eyes had flicked over him, as if unwilling to take in his face, his presence, for any longer than necessary.

The sirens cut through their awkward triangle.

"I'm sorry," Mrs. Marshall said again. "I just heard the screams and called the police." She turned and pushed her cell phone into the back pocket of her jeans, straightening the hem of her Windbreaker. She waved an arm over her head.

Avery's stomach dropped low when she saw the flashing red-and-blue lights attached to the grill of the black GMC pulling into the Marshalls' driveway.

TWENTY-FIVE

As they neared Fletcher's house, the police chief turned on his blinker and gently guided the car to the side of the road. Fletcher could see Avery straightening in the front seat.

"Dad, can you pull over more?"

The chief turned on the emergency hazards. "We're fine where we are Avery. Now…"—he clicked off his seat belt, the release of it like a shot—"care to tell me what you two kids were doing outside of the Marshalls' house? Thank God I was able to call Blount off as backup, or we could have had a standoff."

Avery opened her mouth but her father held up his hand. "If you're going to lie, save it." He turned around in his seat. "Fletcher?"

Fletcher had answered the same questions asked a hundred different ways for Chief Templeton over the last two weeks, but it was terrifying to be questioned while sitting in the back of a police vehicle.

"We were—"

The chief's eyebrows went up. "We?"

"Yeah, Dad, we," Avery cut in. "Fletch and me, we wanted to see Mrs. Marshall."

"Why?"

"We were looking for clues, okay?"

Fletcher could see the back of Chief Templeton's neck go red. "I told you—"

"You stopped your investigation, Dad! What else were we supposed to do? Your impounded Fletcher's car and searched his room and house. No one is out looking for the person who really did this!"

Fletcher could hear the conviction in Avery's voice. He didn't know if Avery was right or wrong anymore. He didn't know if there was a monster out there in the world or in here, in the car.

TWENTY-SIX

Avery's frustration was bubbling. She wanted to scream at both Fletcher and her father. She wanted them to stop talking and actually *do* something. She was tired of her classmates accusing Fletcher of murder and accusing her of being an accomplice. At least her father hadn't heard that rumor yet.

The chief slowed his car in front of Fletcher's house, and Avery caught Fletcher shrinking back in the rearview mirror. His face went weirdly slack. She followed his gaze.

"Hey, Fletch, who's that man in front of the house with your mom?"

Fletcher whispered, "That's my dad."

● ● ●

"Did you know that was Fletcher's dad?" Avery asked.

Her father didn't answer, just shook his head with his jaws clenched together. Avery's stomach shivered.

"Look, Dad, I'm really sorry—"

"Save it."

They were quiet until he pulled into the garage and took

his key from the ignition, killing the engine. Neither of them moved.

"I am so, so disappointed in you, Avery."

Her father didn't yell and didn't even look at her when he said it—and that made it sting more. She couldn't control her tears.

"I was just trying to help."

"I know. Adam was your friend; Fletcher is your friend. But you have no idea what you're getting yourself into, Avy. You just don't. This isn't about little kids and broken bones or baseball or whatever memories you have of those boys. When I say it's police business, it's not because I want to shut you out. It's because I want to protect you. I've had years of police training. You haven't. I thought you were old enough to understand that."

"I am, Dad. But—"

"There are no buts. I can't recuse myself from this case so you're going to have to suck it up and listen to me. I am not happy with you."

"Adam had a bunch of money in his bottom drawer. And he also had knives."

"What?"

"Fletcher is starting to remember things."

"Fletcher remembered that about Adam?"

She opened her mouth and then closed it again, unsure of what to say. "Doesn't that make a difference in your investigation? You know there was a car in the lot that day, and Adam—Adam could have been dealing drugs or something."

"How much money did he have? Did Fletcher know? Was it on Adam when they went for the hike?"

She followed her father out of the car and into the house. "It seemed like a lot of money. A couple thousand dollars at least. I—I mean, Fletcher didn't know if Adam had it on him when they went hiking. But why would Adam need that kind of money walking in the woods?"

"Avery, a couple thousand dollars isn't a huge sum of money."

"I don't have that kind of money stashed in my room! What if he was dealing drugs or something, Dad? He could have had enemies because of that. Or someone could have known that he had cash."

"We don't even know that he was carrying any money when he went off with Fletcher."

Avery grabbed her father's arm and shook it. "But it's a possibility, right? You'll check into it?"

"Yes, honey, and I will." But Avery knew he wouldn't.

• • •

Fletcher's parents didn't say anything when Chief Templeton brought him home, and they stayed silent while they walked into the house, Fletcher in tow. He knew what they were thinking and he didn't care. They had no idea what was going on. They didn't know how he felt with the weight of accusation pushing down on his chest while the whispers told him crazy things and made it hard to concentrate.

They'd never understood him.

Even when they were all together, his family never understood him. They all smiled like someone might snap their picture at any time, but none of them were happy. His mother was always jumpy. His father was hardly home, but when he was, his behavior was aggressive. And Susan…she had been sick since the day she was born. She was older than Fletcher but meek, with slight shoulders and a tiny frame. She was fragile.

Like any younger brother, Fletcher had liked to pester his sister—beheading her dolls, taking her stuff, calling her names. His father called it "brother stuff." His mother would tell him to behave. And Susan would always cry, making everyone feel sorry for her. Still, sometimes he missed her.

"Fletcher?"

His parents were sitting across from each other at the dinner table, holding hands. His mother cleared her throat and straightened her skirt. His father had the look he seemed to always wear—wary, suspicious.

"Sit down, please. And tell us what happened."

Fletcher recounted the same story that he and Avery had shared with Chief Templeton. Afterward, he felt relieved. His father hadn't interrupted him or leaped up from his chair, yelling at him to "tell *the* truth—not *your* truth." That was one of his favorite catchphrases when they all still lived together. He thought Fletcher was a liar. Even though his dad stood up for Fletcher, Susan had always been his favorite. Just the thought of that set Fletcher's teeth on edge.

"We need you to tell us what happened in the woods."

The *pssst, pssst, pssst* whispers were coming back. He closed his eyes and pinched the bridge of his nose. When he opened his eyes again, both parents were staring at him intently.

"Tell us from the beginning, Fletch," his father said sternly. "The truth."

His mother nodded. "We need to hear it. All of it."

• • •

Avery couldn't sleep.

Maybe they were in on it together... Stay away from him, Avy, at least for now... They found Adam. They found his body...

She massaged her temples, trying to connect the important details. If she were an investigator, what would she think? She briefly flashed back to the murder board at the police station and dismissed the idea of riding out there in the middle of the night. Instead she rolled out a piece of paper and took out some markers, slashing a long, black line across the middle of the paper. She started hatching a timeline.

12 o'clock: F&A pull into the parking lot @ Cascade (another car in parking lot)

6:07 p.m.: Dad gets call that Fletch is missing

8:40 p.m. next day: I find Fletch

5:00 a.m.: Talk to Fletch; he remembers nothing

She tapped her pen against her bottom lip and frowned. She didn't have too many details, but it was a start. What she didn't know was who had been with Fletch and Adam on that trail. Avery dropped her pen and flopped backward onto her bed.

"What else, what else, what else?" Her eyes skittered over her walls as if somehow the answer had been there all along, just waiting for her to stumble on it. What she did stumble on was the front page of the newspaper from the day that Fletcher had been found. She stood up and sifted through the stack of newspapers she had kept from each day that Fletch and Adam's case was mentioned.

She scrutinized all of the pictures, looking for anyone suspicious in the crowd, anyone who showed up in multiple shots. Again, thinking of the fact that killers liked to insert themselves into investigations, and if Fletcher was at one of the press conferences or town halls, he would have been a target too.

Avery narrowed her eyes at the grainy picture of the search teams signing in. She recognized pretty much everyone and tossed the page aside. Underneath was another paper, this one bearing the thick, black headline "The Escape" and featuring a school picture of Fletcher, something that wasn't particularly recent because he still had that hint of boyish baby fat in his cheeks and he was smiling. Avery remembered last year's yearbook shot of Fletch. He wasn't smiling but he wasn't frowning either. His eyes focused directly on the camera. His shoulders were slack underneath the oversized T-shirt he wore.

"Not warm and fuzzy enough," Avery guessed.

The other papers reused the same few shots, so she went online to search. There was a shot from her dad's press conference, the chief at the podium caught in midsentence, a cluster of rapt townspeople around him. Fletcher was in the background, nearly hidden under a tree with his bike. Avery flipped to the next image. This one showed a group of nurses and doctors huddled around Fletcher, who sat in a wheelchair, a shy smile on his face. There were balloons and someone was holding out a cake with "Get Well Soon" scrolled in blue icing. It was the day he had been released.

She scrolled through a few more shots until her eyelids grew heavy. The only person who appeared in every picture was Fletcher.

TWENTY-SEVEN

He had to talk to Avery. If he could make her see, she would understand. She was probably the only person who would understand. After last night, it was obvious that his parents didn't. They'd said things to him in nice, soothing tones, but the whispers were so loud that he couldn't concentrate on what his mom and dad were saying.

"They're going to send you away," the whisper hissed. "Your mother sent Susan away to protect her, but they're not going to protect you… No one is going to protect you."

The murmurs stayed in the back of his mind. They gave him a headache.

Fletcher rolled over and picked up the phone.

Avery answered on the second ring. "Fletcher?"

"I need to go back into the woods."

There was a pause and Fletcher counted out the seconds.

"Are you sure?"

Determination pumped through his veins like adrenaline. "If I can get back in the woods, I know I can remember something."

He felt good. He knew it was only a matter of time before this whole thing could be over. He knew he had to be the one who ended it, but he knew Avery would have to help. It had to be now because his parents… He didn't want to think about them.

"Yeah, I'm sure. I've started to remember a few things, but I feel like if I go back there, maybe even to the same spot, I could remember more. Can you come?"

"Now?"

"Yeah."

Avery didn't hesitate. "Of course."

• • •

Avery kicked off the covers and considered what to tell her father. "I'm running off to the woods with Fletcher, the boy you told me to stay away from, and we're going to catch a killer" wasn't going to fly. She dressed quickly and instead penned a note—"Went on a walk with Ellison. Be back in a few hours!" She signed it with smiley faces and hearts to absorb her guilt from lying. She grabbed her orange search-and-rescue jacket and stuffed it in her backpack, then headed outside to wait for Fletcher.

He rolled up almost immediately.

"Did you have to sneak out?" he asked once they hit the main road.

"Depends what you mean by 'sneak.'"

"To sneak. The act of sneaking. To do something in a stealthy or furtive manner."

She looked at him, impressed. "Stealthy and furtive?"

"Dictionary dot com."

"Nice." She flashed a wide smile back, and it was easy for

Fletcher to believe that it was a normal day, that he and Avery were going for a hike in the woods. He'd packed a couple of waters and two peanut-butter sandwiches in his backpack, and then at the last minute, he threw in a half bag of Kettle Chips, an entire sleeve of Oreo cookies, and an apple, just in case she was the healthy type.

The radio hummed in the background. But as they drove farther from town, there came a rustling noise like static. Fletcher batted at his ear, trying to get it to stop.

"You okay?"

"Yeah." Fletcher forced a smile. "Just thought there was a fly or something."

He closed one eye and cocked his head, giving it a sharp shake like a swimmer might do after a dive.

Avery gripped the door handle, nerves ratcheting up as she kept her eyes focused hard on the road. "Fletch, keep your eye on the road! Do you want me to see if the bug has started a colony in there or something?" Tentatively, she unclenched the door handle and scooched closer to Fletcher, as close as her seat belt would allow.

She gently tugged on his earlobe, but he pulled away so hard that his head smacked his side window.

"Omigosh!"

"What are you doing?" His heart was hammering and the whispers had reached a roaring crescendo. If Avery got too close, if she touched him, would she hear the whispers too? Would she know he was crazy—no. Not crazy. He wasn't crazy.

"I'm sorry." She scooted all the way back into her seat, then gripped the shoulder belt tightly.

"No, no. I'm sorry. I didn't realize you were going to—you surprised me is all." He smiled at Avery and she smiled back, her lips pressed together tightly.

"Sorry," she said again, looking at her lap.

They drove the rest of the way to Cascade Mountain in silence. In his mind, Fletcher cursed the whispers, and his own stupidity and weirdness.

"So I thought that if we kind of retraced me and Adam's trail, maybe that would trigger a few memories."

"Yeah," she said, her voice tentative. "That sounds good."

• • •

Fletcher pulled into a parking spot and Avery kicked open the door, squinting up at the sky. The blue had turned to a flat gray, wisps of fog starting to blot out the sun.

"Looks like it might rain later," she said. "We should probably be pretty quick out here."

Fletcher didn't answer.

There was only one car in the parking lot—a busted-up VW van covered in bumper stickers and in dire need of a wash.

"There was a car in the lot when you and Adam came too, right?"

Fletcher nodded, his eyes flicking over the bus. "Yeah, but it was a different car."

"What kind was it?"

He shouldered a backpack from his trunk. She wasn't sure what he had in it, but it looked heavy. "I don't think I remember."

Avery stepped close enough to him that she could smell the clean scent of detergent on his navy-blue Henley. "Think."

He grimaced with annoyance, but Fletcher obliged, closing his eyes and breathing deeply. "I think it was red. No, maroon. A sedan. Not a van."

Avery pulled a notebook from her own backpack and scrawled "maroon" and "sedan."

"Nice notepad, detective."

It was one of her father's that she had pilfered from his office. She smiled and shrugged. "My dad's the chief, but I can't have a 'get out of jail free' card. I figured a free notebook was an acceptable door prize. Anything else you remember about the car?"

Fletcher huffed and Avery wasn't sure if it was from the weight of his pack or because he was tired of her questions.

"No." He shook his head. "Nothing."

"Okay." She slid the notebook into the pocket of her orange search-and-rescue jacket. "You said Adam threw out some trash before you hit the trail."

"I did?"

"Uh-huh. He said that people were jerks, picked up some trash, and then threw it away. Don't you remember telling me that?"

"Sure. Yeah. Of course I do."

Avery turned toward the mouth of the trail. She found Fletcher's hand and squeezed it before letting it go. "Are you sure about this?"

"Yeah, why not?"

"Well, if at any time being here gets to be too much for you, promise me you'll let me know. If you feel uncomfortable, we'll turn around."

Fletcher's nostrils flared. "I said I'm fine, okay? God! It's not like I'm going to snap or anything!"

Avery stared, openmouthed. She couldn't remember ever hearing Fletch raise his voice, let alone yell at her. Now he was huffing, little bits of spittle forming at the corners of his mouth.

"Okay." She instinctively took a step back, wanting to put a little distance between them. "I didn't mean anything by it. I just wanted to let you know that it's cool—"

"I know," Fletcher said, his voice lowered but still agitated. "I know it's cool. Can we just get on with it?"

"Sure." Avery glanced up over his shoulder and Fletcher spun around.

"Is someone behind me?"

She felt the hairs on the back of her neck stand up. "No."

Avery knew that returning to the woods would be traumatic, but why was Fletcher behaving so erratically? He had a sheen of sweat on his forehead even though they hadn't yet taken a single step on the trail.

Give him a break, she said, calming herself. *This has to be hard for him. Think about…* She tried to shut down her mind, but the image was already there. Her father, holding her hand over the center console, the vibration from the engine quaking up her arm.

"Are you sure you want to do this, Avery?"

"Dad, watch the road."

He sighed, his attention focused on his driving. "I know Dr. Rickson thinks this is a good idea, but I'm not so sure."

"You drive this road every day."

She saw the muscle jump against his jaw.

"I don't like it," he said, his voice gravelly.

"You can't keep avoiding it every time I'm in the car."

"I don't mind, Avy."

"I do mind."

Her stomach quivered. It wasn't butterflies; butterflies were too nice for what she was feeling. It was more like bat wings flapping or spider feet stomping.

Her father cracked a window and the heady scent of pine filled the car. It was fresh and spicy, a scent that Avery and her mother used to love. They would tromp through the forest and her mother would throw back her head, open her arms and yell, "Can you smell that, Avs? That's the smell of heaven!"

Heaven. The word stuck in her throat.

"We're almost to the bend," her dad said, slowing the GMC to a crawl, then a stop. When he pulled the keys from the ignition, the silence was overwhelming. She was relieved when the tick-tick-tick of the cooling engine started.

"Do you want to go closer or stay here?" her father asked gently.

Avery's eyes were already fixed. She slid out of the car without answering. With each step she took, she felt like the vise on her heart was squeezing tighter. The scar on the tree was unmistakable. A huge branch had ripped from the trunk, exposing the yellow-white flesh of the tree beneath its bark.

Avery sucked in a shaky breath. Taking another step closer caused physical pain.

Her mother's car had slid into a gully on the side of the road. Tire marks snaked out behind it. A few broken chunks of metal and a shower of broken glass still dotted pine needles and brush. It had been nearly two months; Avery wondered if they would ever get cleaned up, or if the detritus would just become part of the landscape.

The snap of saplings brought Avery back to the trail in the forest. Fletcher was a good ten feet in front of her, whacking at low tree limbs and brush with a stick. She caught up with him, branches snapping beneath her feet, and Fletcher turned, stick held out in front of him like a weapon. He was breathing hard again—small, shallow breaths.

Avery jumped back. "Whoa!"

Fletcher tapped the tip of the stick on the ground. "Sorry. You surprised me."

"Next time I'll wear a bell," she said under her breath.

They walked along in silence again. Every few feet he'd pause, eyes darting from side to side. Avery thought he was just trying to remember the way he and Adam had come, but as they went deeper into the forest, she wasn't so sure.

She licked her lips. "So, anything coming to you?"

"You miss your mom?" He didn't stop or look at her, just kept walking.

Avery was taken aback. "Yeah, of course I do."

"My mom's weird."

Avery nodded, walking a foot behind Fletcher. "She seems okay."

"She thinks I did it."

Avery's stomach plummeted, her chest tight. "She thinks you…"

"Killed Adam." He stopped, then turned, a loose smile on his lips. "Everyone thinks I did it."

"Who do you mean by *everyone*?" Sweat beaded her upper lip. "That's not what I think."

He looked her up and down, that weird smile still playing at the corners of his lips. Avery crossed her arms and straightened with bravado she didn't feel. She felt vulnerable. Exposed.

"I don't think you killed Adam, Fletch. I know you too well. I know you would never do something like that."

He narrowed his eyes. The air between them crackled with electricity.

"Let's keep walking."

• • •

Fletcher didn't know why Avery kept falling behind him. The incline wasn't that steep and they weren't walking that fast.

She is scared. She is scared of me. The thought burned in his gut. Why should she be afraid of him?

Killer…killer…killer, the whispers chanted.

He tried to brush them away but they were persistent: *Killer… killer…kill her.*

"Shut up!"

Avery looked at him, startled. "I didn't say anything."

Embarrassment burned up Fletcher's spine, flushing the back of his neck. "Sorry, Avery. I didn't mean…I didn't mean anything."

They were nearing the clearing by the gully.

"My God, Fletch. Dude, you've got to see this…"

"Did you hear that?" Fletcher asked suddenly.

Avery looked around, her forehead wrinkled in confusion. "Hear what?"

The adrenaline was coming fast and hard now, pumping through his veins. "Adam. It sounded like Adam."

Avery took a step back, her eyes saucers as she shook her head from side to side. "No, Fletch. I didn't hear anything. Maybe we should head back. I think this may have been a bad idea."

Why was she doing that? Didn't she want to find Adam?

What happened to Adam?

He watched his own arm dart out like a venomous snake and grab Avery's wrist. "Come on. Come on, let's go."

She followed, but after a few steps, she shook him off. "I think this was a bad idea, Fletch. I'm going to go back."

"No! You can't!" Fletcher stared into Avery's eyes. "We can't."

"Fletch—"

"You found me once, Avery. Please don't let me get lost again."

Avery nodded slowly. "Okay."

TWENTY-EIGHT

Fletch was acting weird.

Really weird.

His eyes were wild, and he jumped at every sound: a squirrel in the brush, his own foot snapping a twig. He was sweating profusely, though his breathing was more subdued. Still, something was wrong.

Fletcher stopped abruptly.

"What happened, Fletch? What happened out here?"

His lower lip started to tremble. He flapped his hand by his ear again. It almost sounded as if he was humming.

"Fletcher?"

He pointed to the ground. "We were here. Me and Adam."

Avery's palms went clammy against the notebook in her hand. "Go on."

"He's bad, Avery. He's really, really bad." He cocked his head, eyes still flashing primitively, and pressed his finger against his lips. "He's probably listening right now."

"Who's listening? Who are you talking about?"

It sounded like Fletcher said "Adam." But before she could ask, he reached out and gripped Avery by her wrist, yanking her along with him deeper into the gully. Enormous redwoods were all around them, branches crosshatched over their heads and blocking out the sunlight. The deep pine scent was claustrophobic. Avery dug in her heels.

"Stop it, Fletch. You know that Adam is dead."

Fletcher looked at her. He blinked. "He had to."

She pulled her arms free. "He had to what?"

"Die, Avery. Adam had to die."

Ice water exploded in Avery's veins. "Who said he had to die?"

Fletcher took another step toward her. Avery could smell him, the clean scent of detergent now smothered by sweat and dirt. He leaned close, his lips brushing against her ear. "*They* did."

Avery's heart slammed against her ribs. "Who are *they*?"

Fletcher licked his lips. "Do you miss your mom, Avery?"

The air went still.

"You already asked me that."

He smiled, a toothy, easy smile that shot terror through her. "My mom is always watching me."

He turned and began walking down the trail, winding deeper into the woods.

"Hey, Fletch, let's just—"

Fletcher paused and kicked at a pinecone at the edge of the trail. "My mom is always watching me, Avery. I think…I think she does it for them."

"That's normal, Fletch. My dad watches me like a hawk."

Fletcher cocked an eyebrow. "Does he?"

"Yeah." Avery knew it was a lie but suddenly she felt exposed, felt the need to cover herself. She wasn't exactly regretting coming out here with Fletcher, but she was no longer excited about it either.

"I think your father watches everyone." Another turn, another few feet into the forest. "He doesn't pay that much attention to you. He wasn't even there that night."

"What night?"

"The night all your windows were opened."

"He was working."

"He wasn't there to see the way you looked when you came down the stairs." He dragged his tongue over his lower lip, smiling faintly. His eyes were distant, like he was seeing something other than the trees around them. "You looked like one of those cops on TV." He mimed holding a gun close to his chest, the way she had held her flashlight, as he sidestepped down a grade. "You looked so beautiful."

Fletcher locked his gaze on Avery. She shivered. "You were there?"

He pressed a finger against her pursed lips and shushed her. "They were there."

"Who are they?" Avery said, unable to keep the exasperation out of her voice. "You're scaring me, Fletcher. Who are they and why did they want Adam to die and…and…"—her voice faltered even as she tried to pump in false bravado—"why were they at my house? How did they get in?"

Fletcher leaned close to Avery. "I let them in."

• • •

Fletcher didn't want to be in the forest. He'd thought he would be able to remember things, but the same fingers of darkness had reached out to him the second he set foot on the trail. They inched closer. But he couldn't let Avery see…

He stomped down the whispers as best he could, but even then they reached back for him. One voice at first, then another, then the one he couldn't stand: Adam's. Adam's was soft. Adam's was sinister.

"Fletcher…" It was back again, hissing in his ear. "You remember what happened. You remember what happened out here… You remember what you did…"

"No, I don't," he forced out between gritted teeth.

Avery stopped walking. "Did you say something?"

Fletcher ignored Avery. The throbbing in his head matched the rise and fall of Adam's whispered voice. He swatted as if the voice was a gnat in his ear and it laughed, enjoying toying with him.

Adam's voice lured him farther and farther down the trail until the sunlight became mottled and sparse, blotted out by the canopy of old-growth trees knitted together more the deeper they went.

Avery kept talking, telling Fletcher she wanted to go back. He did too, but Adam's voice—and something else—compelled him to keep moving. Maybe inside the forest he could find peace. Maybe if he went deep enough, they would leave him alone. The temperature started to drop and Avery wanted to know about *them* again. Fletcher ignored her and kept moving.

• • •

Avery had her phone out, holding it up until a few meager bars populated the screen. "I'm going to call my dad. He can send his guys in here and they can walk with you."

Fletcher turned, his eyes wild, his lips twisted into a snarl. He was on Avery in a heartbeat, his hand knocking the phone from hers.

"No!"

The phone sailed out of her hand, skittering down the ridge and disappearing somewhere on the forest floor.

"What did you do that for?"

"You can't call him! He's going to send me away. You're going to ask him to send me away."

Fletcher's face was a deep red and sweat raced over his brow. He dug both hands into his hair and gripped, baring his teeth. "I'm not crazy. I'm *not* crazy!"

Avery's bottom lip started to tremble.

"I'm not crazy," Fletcher said slowly.

Avery licked her lips and nodded, her mind racing, trying to remember if she'd ever heard that her father had been in a similar situation. *What would he do?*

"Of course you're not crazy, Fletcher. I never said that."

"Your dad will take me away."

Avery's eyes focused on Fletcher's wild ones, her every muscle tensed and ready to run. "He won't take you away. He just wants to help you like I do."

"No, no." Fletcher shook his head. "You can't help me. You're on their side. You're one of them. Adam…Adam was one of them too."

"Fletch—"

"That's why he had to die, Avery. That's why I had to kill him."

Fire sparked somewhere low in Avery's gut and singed every inch of her. She'd heard wrong. She had to have heard wrong. Evil was other people, not someone she knew. Not her friend. "You killed Adam?"

Fletcher leaned down low, legs spread as though he would pounce at any moment.

"Had to," Fletcher said.

Suddenly, he straightened up and shimmied the backpack from his back. It landed with a thump.

If he turns around, I'll run, she told herself. *I'll make a break for it, back to the trailhead, back to the car.*

But Fletcher had the keys. And even if he didn't, Avery couldn't drive.

She heard him unzip the backpack and rifle through it; from the corner of her eye she spied him removing two bottles of water. She saw the car keys slip down and disappear at the bottom of the pack.

I could lock myself in the car.

"My dad was going to send me away," Fletcher said, opening one of the water bottles and taking a big gulp. "He told my mom I didn't belong out in the world. Not after what I did to Susan."

Avery snapped to attention. "Susan?"

"My sister." He spat on the ground.

"What happened to your sister?"

Fletcher's eyes pinned Avery's. "Who told you?"

He roared and Avery covered her ears.

"Who told you about Susan?" Fletcher demanded again.

And then, *smack!*

Avery reeled. The slap against her cheek burned fiery hot. "You hit me!"

"Did they tell you?" He had his hands on her shoulders, his fingers digging into her flesh as he shook her. "What did they tell you?"

• • •

The voices were growing more insistent. Whispers turned to screams that echoed in his mind, warning him. Avery was one of them. She wanted to put Fletcher away, wanted to lock him up and throw away the key.

He could feel her hot flesh under his palms, and that almost reminded him that she was the Avery Templeton who believed he wasn't crazy. But then the voices began to separate and disappear, slipping from his head and out into the forest. He shoved Avery away when the first one flashed by him, a thick, black blur, running.

His head was hurting and he couldn't stop thinking of Susan and Adam, and now Avery. He was in trouble. If he didn't get them, they were going to get him. The voices told him to fight. The people in the forest—the ones darting behind trees just before he could see them, before he could figure out who they were—told him to kill her. They told him it was only a matter of time before Avery's father came and took him away.

• • •

Avery's feet tangled on Fletcher's backpack, and she hit the ground with a thud. She could feel her palms shredding on the pebbles, and she shrieked when the weight of the backpack pulled her ankle, quirking it at a weird angle.

"Ow! Fletcher!"

But he wasn't paying any attention to her. His lips were moving, but he wasn't making a sound. He just turned in fast, jerky motions, looking at the trees, as though something was going to jump out at him.

"Why are you acting like this? What is wrong with you?"

"It's Adam," Fletcher said. He didn't seem to be speaking to Avery, but she wasn't sure *who* he was speaking to. "It was Adam. Adam this whole time. He's trying to kill me. They are all trying to kill me."

Avery extracted her foot from the backpack strap and massaged her ankle. It didn't seem to be broken but was swelling against her boot. "Fletch, you have to stop—" Avery stopped in midsentence when the flash of something silver sliding out of the backpack caught her eye.

A pocketknife.

About the size of her palm, about the size of the imprint left in Adam's knife case.

"Fletch, how do you have this?"

He turned and blinked at her, his eyes wide like saucers. They locked gazes for a beat and then Fletcher launched himself forward, going after the knife.

Avery snatched it and shoved it in her pocket, but that didn't deter Fletcher. He jumped on top of her, clawing at her arms, pulling on the pockets of her jeans.

"Stop! Stop!"

Avery struggled, adrenaline blocking out the pain she knew she should have felt as she tried to peel Fletcher off her.

"You're going to kill me! They tried to warn me!" Fletcher was yelling in her face, so close that little bits of spit hit Avery's cheeks.

"Fletcher, stop, it's me! It's Avery! I'm your friend!"

Fletcher growled down at her and stopped moving, blinking as though recognizing her for the first time. Avery panted, her heart pounding against her rib cage. "We're friends."

Fletcher sat back on his haunches, still on top of Avery. He seemed to be thinking, considering what she was saying. Tears flooded her eyes.

"Is this what you did to Adam? Did you—did you do it?"

She could feel the rage crash over him. She slid her feet underneath herself and bucked Fletcher off before he could grab her. His fist slammed into the earth a half inch from her ear, and Avery crab walked away and got to her feet. Fletcher dove for her, his hand grazing her ponytail, grabbing a fistful of hair.

"Adam had to die! Adam had to die! They made me do it. I had to!"

TWENTY-NINE

Avery took off running. Each time her foot hit the ground, pain exploded in her ankle, sending shock waves through her body. Fletcher killed Adam. And now Fletcher was going to kill her. She could hear him running behind her, sloppily, stomping though mounds of dried brush and leaves that she skirted.

"Avery!" Fletcher's voice was nearly unrecognizable, a shrill tear through the silent forest. "Avery, get back here!"

Her heart was hammering; she felt like she was breathing in broken glass. The grove of trees opened on a meadow, streaks of yellow sunlight breaking through the graying sky. She teetered on the edge. There was no place to hide in the meadow. She paused, her blood rushing.

There was no sound.

She didn't hear Fletcher stomping through the grass. She didn't hear him yelling for her.

Maybe he stopped. Maybe he gave up.

She folded over, hands on knees, greedily sucking in air through lungs that felt desperate.

"Avery!" Fletcher's voice echoed. It bounced in front of her and behind her, came from all sides.

"Where is he?" she whispered to herself.

The silence was more terrifying than fighting Fletcher. He could be anywhere. Avery hugged the tree line, doing her best to stay hidden behind the brush and trees. She picked her steps carefully but was sure the thundering power of her heart would give away her location. Her heart pounding in her ears was all she could hear. She was sure that Fletcher could hear it too.

• • •

The whispers stopped abruptly. As if a switch had been flipped. Fletcher was deep in the forest, alone, wrapped in the desolate silence. He didn't know where Avery was. Why would she leave him?

"Avery?"

He took a few steps and her name echoed back to him again and again. She didn't respond. Fletcher couldn't remember which direction he was going or which way he had come. And he couldn't remember where Adam was.

Adam.

The memory—grabbing Adam, landing the first blow—came crashing back and Fletcher doubled over, the weight of it like a swift punch in the gut.

"Hey, Fletch, you've got to see this, man."

Fletch hiked up the slope to where Adam was standing. He was already winded from running, and now his calves were burning and cramping.

"What is it?"

Adam grinned and gave him a shove. Fletcher tripped over his feet and a hunk of dead wood and rolled down into the gully.

"Dude, I'm sorry… I didn't mean to—" There was a look on Adam's face that Fletcher couldn't identify.

Fletch slid a few more inches and then landed on something hard at the bottom of the pit. It poked at the bare skin on his back. He frowned and tried to push himself up, away from what was jabbing him.

It was a skull. An animal with a mouth full of teeth and sun-bleached incisors. Its eye sockets stared up at Fletcher. He screamed, his feet unable to gain traction to move him away. He rose a few inches and slid back down, the hideous skull grinning at him, staring at him.

He could hear Adam laughing, the sound echoing through the forest and filling his ears. But something cut through the sound. A whisper, the faintest whisper. He felt himself start to tremble.

"Who's there?" he asked, his voice small and breathy.

Adam looked down on Fletcher, hands on hips, grinning. "Dude, who are you talking to?"

Fletcher looked around him. There were more bones. Each one was sun-bleached and bare.

"Dude, you're crazy. Come on." Adam lay on the ground, swinging an arm toward Fletcher. Fletcher tried to reach for Adam's hand, but his sneakers slipped and he went down again. Again, Adam laughed. Again, the skull was in front of him, mouth gaping, eyes scrutinizing. Then it whispered in his ear: "He's making fun of you, Fletcher. He hates you. Make him quiet. Make him quiet like Susan. They're both coming to get you."

"Stop screwing around. I don't want to be here all day," Adam said.

Fletcher remembered reaching for Adam. He remembered their fingers touching. He remembered what the skull whispered to him. Adam pulled him up and they were face-to-face.

The first blow made him shake. He remembered the fire in his arm, the way it shot out even though he couldn't remember thinking he should strike. He thought his hand was broken. He remembered the sickening sound of bone hitting bone, the way Adam's head shot back from his neck.

He remembered the whispers cheering him on.

• • •

"Dammit!" Avery muttered, feeling the tears at the edges of her eyes. If Fletcher didn't catch her, she would die in the woods. She was too far away from the Cascade trail they had come down. Everything looked the same—tall trees, dead bushes, mountains of pine needles. She had no idea which direction to turn.

Why is Fletcher doing this?

She dropped her head in her hands and pulled her knees up to her chest, Adam's knife poking into her thigh.

He was going to kill me.

• • •

There was a meadow in front of him. It was like a mirage from one of those old cartoons, a lush oasis in the middle of the desert. But he didn't know where Avery was. The whispers told him he had to find her; they throbbed with the needling pain behind his eyes.

Find her, find her, find her…

"No." He said it out loud, trying to shake the whisper from his head. "No." He was halfway lucid now, somewhere on the edge between his waking self and the other self, the one that came back after Dr. Palmer tried to push it down.

"Schizophrenia, Fletcher. It's called schizophrenia."

He remembered being strapped down in the hospital, his mother brushing the hair from his forehead as her mouth rolled around the word. He remembered that someone had attacked Susan. That his mother whispered when she thought he was asleep: "He's my son, and I'm not going to leave him here."

"You're picking one child over the other. He's dangerous. He can't be in the same house as Susan," his father whispered in response.

"He's just a little boy. He didn't know what he was doing."

"You're insane. He attacked Susan. We have to protect our daughter."

"I'm going to protect my son." His mother—strong, defiant.

• • •

Avery held her breath. She could see Fletcher. She prayed he didn't see her. He was murmuring things, flicking at his ear with those same awkward movements. She watched him brush the hair from his forehead, matted with sweat, and look around. She watched as he pivoted so that his body was facing her hiding spot. Avery didn't dare look up at him.

"Avery?" Fletcher's voice was tremulous and soft. Haunting. "Avery, I'm sorry. I didn't mean to scare you."

He took a step toward her, leaves crackling under his sneakers. Avery dug her teeth into her bottom lip, sure that her body was betraying her: blood pulsing, heart beating, breath whooshing through her barely parted lips. Fletcher must have heard her. She clenched her teeth as she started to tremble. Her thighs were aching as she hunched down.

Fletcher took another step.

Avery's muscles cramped.

She let the cry die in her chest, but her knee couldn't hold, brushing against a branch.

Fletcher's eyes cut right to her. His lips began to move, a wide, slow smile spreading across his lips. "Hi, Avery."

"Please, Fletcher. Please don't hurt me. I want to help you."

He cocked his head, the silence between them weighted and eerie. "I would never want to hurt you."

• • •

The whispers broke in, the chorus going from a gentle murmur to a brain-bashing thunder. Fletcher pressed his palms against his ears and pinched his eyes closed.

"Shut up, shut up, shut up!"

• • •

Avery's body took over. She sprang up to run. Pain, like a live wire, shot up from her ankle and she crumbled. Avery heard herself squeal as she went down, while Fletcher's hand closed around her other ankle. Avery clawed at the ground, her nails breaking in the dirt. Fletcher yanked her closer, stepping hard on the small of her back. Heat broke within her, the pain rolling from her low back around to her belly, stabbing and nauseating. Avery kicked and flopped like a fish out of water and Fletcher toppled, landing behind her with a loud *oof.*

Avery was up and running again.

She could hear Fletcher behind her, stomping through the

waist-high grasses as she cut across the meadow. He was yelling for her in that same primitive, throaty voice that she barely recognized. She flung a look over her shoulder. This Fletcher, the one who tailed her with his teeth bared and his eyes narrowed, was someone she didn't know. This Fletcher terrified her.

Avery reached the lip of forest on the other side of the meadow, and recognition hit her: this was the part of the forest she and her mother had walked in. She knew there was a burned-out tree and she vaulted for it, sliding at the same time a clap of thunder shook the sky. She dipped into the tree just as the sky opened up. Silver-gray rain came down in torrents.

Fletcher called out to her again, but his voice was sucked away by the sheeting rain. Avery could see him standing a few feet in front of her, head upturned as the water splashed onto his forehead and over his cheeks.

"Get back here, Avery! Get back here!"

Avery glanced up at the rain and back down at her orange search-and-rescue jacket. It was made to be seen. She slid out of it, trembling against the bone-soaking rain, and balled it up, rolling it as carefully as she could down the gentle slope she had come up. It stopped at the base of a giant redwood ten feet away, one of the sleeves trailing like a beacon. She prayed that Fletcher would see it.

• • •

She had to be here.

Get her, get her, get her, the whispers chanted. *Can't you do anything right?*

Fletcher looked up, unsure when the rain had started.

Where was he? What was he doing?

He blinked, pushing his feet through the dirt as it turned to mud.

"Avery?"

His mind raced. They were hiking. They had come out here to find Adam. No, Adam was dead. He remembered that.

Clues.

They had come out looking for clues to jog his memory.

And now Avery was lost.

A sob lodged in his throat. *How did Avery get lost?* He called her name again, fear fluttering inside him. "Avery, are you out here?"

What if she had fallen or slipped? The rain was already pooling at his feet, the mud making a sucking sound as he tried to walk. She could be stuck or hurt. Blood thundered in his ears, the only thing he could hear over the rush of rain. There was water in his eyes, rolling over his cheeks. He wasn't sure if it was raindrops or tears.

"Avery?"

He turned again and saw a slice of bright orange behind a tree. Her search-and-rescue jacket.

"*Avery!*" Fletcher rushed toward her, grinning like a madman, so glad that he had found her. Only it wasn't her. It was just her coat. Fletcher's chest constricted.

"Oh God. Oh God, oh God, oh God." What had happened to Avery?

He whirled when he heard her grunt.

• • •

Avery didn't have any other choice.

She fished Adam's knife from her pocket, folded out the blade, and gripped the handle in her palm. She knew where she was. She remembered the formation of the trees, the burned-out stump—she remembered that just a few feet from her, there was a road. They always stopped at the burned-out tree because her mother hated the road. "It's like an ugly slice right through heaven," she would say as they picnicked under the trees.

The only thing between Avery and the safety of the road was Fletcher.

• • •

Avery grunted and Fletcher turned, relief crashing over him. He saw her emerge from the safety of a burned-out stump. He ran for her, thankful. He wanted to hold her. He wanted to kiss her. He hadn't realized how worried he had been. He ran to her, and her eyes widened in terror. *What had happened? Why was she scared?*

He closed the distance between them, but suddenly there was a severe pain in his thigh. It felt like his kneecap went slack, his hips sliding.

In his mind's eye, he saw his whole skeleton falling into a heap of Halloween bones. Instinctively, his hands went to the source of the pain. His fingers were warm and sticky. He was covered in blood.

Fletcher stared at the handle of the knife. It was the same knife that Adam had given him to hold on to before they walked down the trail. The blade was plunged hilt-deep in his muscle.

He didn't understand. "Avery?"

• • •

Avery stabbed Fletcher. She had no other choice. She ran past him, leaving the knife sticking out of his thigh. Tears clouded her vision. *Get to the road, get to the road, get to the road.*

The rain was steady now, creating rivulets of mud and water. But up ahead, Avery could see headlights on the road. She dug her fingers and the toes of her boots into the mud and pushed herself up, her ankle screaming in protest the entire time. The pain was thrumming all the way up her leg now, begging her not to walk. But she couldn't stop. Fletcher would be behind her—maybe more slowly than before, but he would come after her.

Fletcher is your friend! You stabbed your friend!

No, she told herself, *Fletcher is a murderer.*

Avery's fingertips grazed asphalt just as she heard movement behind her. She could barely make out Fletcher's voice calling her name, the sound half muffled by the rain.

She launched herself the last few feet until her feet met pavement. She pushed her way to standing and darted a few feet, then froze, her entire body paralyzed.

The tree was in front of her. The one with the gash, the scar of her mother's car burned into the trunk. Her stomach turned over on itself, and the bile itched at the back of her throat.

Headlights blinded her.

A horn wailed through the sheets of rain.

Tires squealed, the yellow streaks of light washing over her.

She couldn't move.

Avery didn't know what she felt first: the impact, the terror, or the asphalt cutting through her skin as she skittered across it. The last things she remembered were the ugly sound her head made when it hit the ground and someone calling her name.

Then everything went dark.

THIRTY

A haloed yellow glow throbbed behind Avery's eyelids.

"It looks like she's waking up."

There was a swirl of sounds: beeps and a weird whoosh of air. Slowly, slowly, a face came into view.

"Dad?"

"Oh thank God, Avery. Thank God."

He collapsed on her, gathering her in a tender hug. "What happened?"

There were tears in her father's eyes. "You don't remember?"

She blinked. "Fletcher—Fletch and I went into the woods." She felt herself blanch. "He—he came after me. He said I had to die."

Chief Templeton squeezed Avery's hand. "Fletcher is very, very sick, honey."

Tears pooled on her lower lashes. "He killed Adam. How did I—?" She looked around the hospital room. "Why am I in the hospital? How did I get here?"

"You ran into the street. Fletcher pushed you out of the way."

"How do you know that? There was no one else out there."

"I didn't. It was Officer Blount. He was the one driving."

"Did Mrs. Carroll tell you about Fletcher?"

"No. Fletcher told us about his mother."

Avery sat up. "What?"

"Honey, she was the one who drove you off the road on your bike. She vandalized Fletcher's locker and her own house."

"I don't understand."

"Fletcher has schizophrenia. His father and sister live in a different house because Fletcher attacked his sister when he was eleven. Mrs. Carroll knew that it had to have been Fletcher who murdered Adam, but she couldn't bear the thought. She didn't want to lose her son. She thought if she could drive suspicion away from him, that—" He shrugged. "I don't know what she thought. But I do know I should have listened to you. Your theory was pretty good."

"My theory? Dad, I was completely wrong about Fletcher."

"Sort of. He had a psychotic break. He didn't really know what he was doing when he went after Adam or you. He's going to jail, but he's going to get help there."

Emotions crashed over Avery—she was sad, terrified, exhausted. Adam was dead. Fletcher was going to jail. She felt sorry for him, her friend, sitting alone behind bars. *But he had killed Adam,* she reminded herself. *And he tried to kill me.* Still, it didn't make sense—no part of it seemed right or simple or easy. No part of life felt that way anymore.

"I'm talking about his mother," Chief Templeton went on. "That's the part you got right. You told me she acted strangely and that I should look into it. I didn't listen. I should have." He stroked the back of Avery's hand with his thumb. "You're a pretty decent detective, Templeton."

Even with all the hospital equipment and the sterile walls of the room, Avery felt herself warm. "You're not so bad yourself, Chief."

ACKNOWLEDGMENTS

It takes a village to write a book and this one is no exception. Special thanks to mega-agents Amberly Finarelli and Andrea Hurst for making me feel like family, and to editor Annette Pollert-Morgan for taking a chance on me. As always, thanks to the unstoppable Sourcebooks team for their unyielding awesome. Thanks to Andrew Hensley, MD, for pointing me in the right direction to research mental illness and to Lee Lofland for always providing me access to the best and brightest in law enforcement, namely Marco, Stan, Andy, Rick, and of course, Dr. Love. Thank you Graham Haworth for making me breathe and Lynn Cotner for making me laugh. Thanks to everyone over at Wattpad for their enthusiasm and support of all my works, and an extra-special thanks to all those readers who wrote and cheered me along the way: I wouldn't—couldn't—do this without you.